Haunted House and Other Strange Tales

Haunted House and Other Strange Tales

Katherine Kerestman

Foreword by S. T. Joshi

Hippocampus Press

New York

Published by Hippocampus Press
P.O. Box 641, New York, NY 10156.
www.hippocampuspress.com

Cover design by Dan Sauer, dansauerdesign.com.
Hippocampus Press logo designed by Anastasia Damianakos.

First Edition
1 3 5 7 9 8 6 4 2

ISBN 978-1-61498-453-5 (paperback)
ISBN 978-1-61498-455-9 (ebook)

Contents

Foreword

Katherine Kerestman has been writing fiction for only a few years, but her scholarly and academic credentials go back several decades. She has charmingly delineated her own perspective on life as follows: "In the 1660s, I would have been burned at the stake for being a witch. In the 1760s, I would have been committed to Bedlam. In the 1860s, I would have been consigned to the role of old maid housekeeper (unpaid) for a male relation in need of domestic help. Mercifully, I grew up in the 1960s." In the realm of weird fiction, H. P. Lovecraft and Bram Stoker are among her chief influences; but other weird phenomena, ranging from witch-haunted Salem to *Dark Shadows* to *Twin Peaks,* have also nurtured her imagination. An avid traveler, she has written *Creepy Cat's Macabre Travels* (2020), wherein she has roamed both the Old World and the New World in quest of strangeness. And the title of that book testifies to both her devotion to felines and her awareness of the fundamental weirdness of that enigmatic species.

All these elements can be found in the compressed tales in this volume. Mastery of the short-short story takes a special set of skills on the author's part. Such a form requires an unusually intense application of Poe's strictures on the "unity of effect," whereby every word of a story contributes to its denouement. The short-short story—sometimes designated as a prose poem or (in modern parlance) as "flash fiction"—is uniquely suited to weird fiction, because the meticulous build-up of realistic details can be dispensed with, in exchange for the sudden irruption of the weird or supernatural and the characters' frenzied reactions to it.

In story after story, Kerestman manifests her adeptness at the abbreviated narrative, whether it be set in the past (where she utilizes her knowledge of archaic English to evoke prior eras in a faultlessly accurate prose idiom) or in our own seemingly mundane age, where the weird can burst upon us when we least expect it—checking into a hotel, taking a walk in the woods, browsing in a bookstore, coming upon a stranger in a museum. And the poems scattered throughout this volume testify to Kerestman's ability to manipulate an even more condensed and concentrated form of expression for the purpose of inciting terror.

All this is not to say that Kerestman cannot also work successfully in the longer tale: her novella *Lethal* was published in 2023 by PsychoToxin Press, and other of her tales have appeared in magazines, anthologies, and online venues. But her unique ability to infuse strangeness into the compact mode of the short-short story should be a lesson to us all that, in the hands of a gifted artist, less truly can be more.

—S. T. JOSHI

Gothic Tales

Lenore

It was well past midnight. I had just returned home from Sir James Crypt-Cheswick's renowned Christmas revel. Crypt-Cheswick Hall is a morbid, brooding grey stone edifice constructed in the neo-Gothic style. Gargoyles on the ramparts peer luridly down upon approachers. A black pennant waves from one of the crenellated towers. The details are so complete that even the corners are crumbling.

The great stone hall was aglow. A great blaze roared in the cavernous fireplace. The hearth was flanked by stern-countenanced stone angels who stood guard—as the archangels must have stood who guarded the gates of Paradise to bar the first lovers from the abode of their former bliss. Countless candles burned in the heavy wrought-iron chandeliers suspended overhead from thick wrought-iron chains. And the flickering of the myriad candle flames from the dozens of candelabra arrayed around the room created a hypnotic, kaleidoscopic effect. Banqueting tables were weighted with delicacies of beast and fowl, confectioner and vintner. The air was perfumed by exotic scents wafting from hothouse flowers and mingling with the smoke of cigars.

The guests, all intoxicated bon vivants, were laughing gaily, dancing wildly. The straight-backed men all wore white tie and tails. The ladies were most exquisite, the brilliants among their delicious curls reflecting the candlelight, their soft pliant warmth cruelly coerced by whalebone into shapes for pleasing men. As one bent to kiss a lady's hand, one's eyes must perforce have been beguiled upward to follow the tantalizing flesh emerging from the upper end of her glove. My moustache twitches at the recollection. The festive hall was an ocean of rising and falling décolletage—ebbing and flowing from the efforts of corseted ladies to waltz, their whalebone obliging them to labor all the more for their breath, engendering quite gratifying emotions in this observer. Sir James had outdone himself this Yule.

When I returned home, I handed my coat and hat to my butler and sate before the fire in my chamber, spent by a surfeit of pleasure. I grew tired and mused. Although dawn was approaching, sleep evaded me. I picked up some of my favorite books of necromancy and alchemy. Not long after thumbing through dusty vellums of forgotten lore I began to doze in my chair. A raven attracted by the light of my fire to an alcove of the house began to peck at my window. I awoke and drowsily began to think of Lenore.

It had been a midnight in December such as this. Lenore was the most delightful of beautiful women. She was tall, with an elegant form and a captivating way of swaying her bustled gown as she walked—nay, glided—by. Her blue eyes danced. The finely shaped brows rose on her forehead when she laughed. She smiled for me. She laughed for me. She was devoted to me.

I thrilled to the desires she inflamed in me. I could scarcely keep my seat with the titillation of my imagination when I touched her warm, pink flesh. I could scarcely heed her words when influenced by the music of her voice and the gleam of her eye. The nearness of her body almost drove me to distraction. When I inhaled her perfume, I came close to madness. Our wedding day was to be the first of the new year. The time had come.

I decided, after careful consideration of alternatives, upon small, repeated doses of deadly nightshade, which I placed in her sherry. This restorative I pressed upon her each night as we parted. I carefully made certain that our last kiss took place before she drank her cordial; and after she had swallowed it, I bade her good night, pressing my trembling lips only upon her fingers.

Each night I returned to my love, to see the blossoms in her cheeks becoming lilies and the sparkle in her eyes diminishing. Every evening she rejoiced in my arrival, which joy she expressed in a more muted fashion than hitherto. She ceased to laugh, but still struggled to smile for me, assuring me she would be well again for our wedding day. Her flesh lost its warmth and became pale and cool. The glow deserted her countenance.

On the last night she took to her bed. I sent the nurse away, saying I would sit with her. Before the maid retired, I asked her to put more logs on the fire and lay by some absinthe. I smoothed my love's feverish, damp brow with my palm and tenderly kissed her forehead.

I sat in the large chair by the bed and took up a paper and quill and began writing. I am never so inspired to great work as by the vision of a dying woman, especially a lovely woman who is tender-hearted. It was the last night of December. A gale was blowing, the shutters rattling against the wall. A black bird pecked at the window trying to gain entrance into the firelit bedchamber where Lenore lay dying.

I watched her grimace in pain. Even as delirium set in I observed her efforts to break through the fog of her senses and see me more clearly. She tried to tell me she loved me, but her throat would not make the sounds.

I scratched feverishly on my paper: "Once upon a midnight dreary." My blood was rising, nerves afire as I watched the life ebb from my cherished one. I included the bird at the window in my poem and imagined a dialogue between us about my Lenore. Oh, this was going to be a masterpiece. I asked Lenore was that not so, but she gave no answer.

Invitation to *Danse*

Business was brisk at the apple-seller's cart, where the assiduous minions of courtly ladies in costly brocade silk dresses, the flared sleeves of which reached down to their mud-splattered slippers, in their quest for their mistresses' refreshment were jostled by a group of country yokels in threadbare tunics, the necks of which were clutched in their work-roughened fingers in a futile effort to ward off the bitter chill of All-Hallows Eve; but the apple-vendor's trade did not begin to compare with the commerce of the tavern-keeper at whose door a noisy group were vying for tankards of the soul-numbing elixir that was sold there. The temple of Dionysus was wedged in the shadow of a daunting cathedral, from whose noble summit a single stained-glass rose window glared disapprovingly upon the milling mass of the faithful who were filling every paving stone of the plaza below.

The Eye of God? or the Evil Eye? the Duchesse Antonia whispered wickedly into the ear of her brother-in-law. She was seated at the right hand of the Duc, upon a sumptuous throne decorated with ormolus of gold, which had been raised off the ground by means of a pennant-festooned platform, in order to sequester those who occupied the places closest to God in the divine schemata from contact with the rabble; her husband's younger brother (and heir) occupied the chair on her other side. Antonia looked around, to ascertain that no clerical agent had eavesdropped upon her indiscreet and sacrilegious attempt at humor—a circumstance that could have sped them to the gallows and a premature final reward. The stone-paved plaza that fronted the cathedral was bounded on three of its sides by snaking rows of narrow, three-story frame dwellings whose doors opened directly onto the street, so that if a person failed to look both ways when emerging from his front door he risked stepping into the path of a pedestrian or a coach. Throughout the city, crisscrossed, constricted, and congested mud lanes were hemmed in on both sides by rows of high, thin houses, the second-floor windows of which met above the streets, creating a Minotaur's maze of partially covered walkways that dashed any hope a pedestrian might cherish of seeing the sun which his faith had taught him to believe still reigned in the firmament.

The emphatic clamoring of enormous bells brought about the shifting of the redolent mass of humanity nearer to the cathedral itself, where, before its massive, brass-and-timber doors, a stage had been set up, on which a company of jugglers dressed in particolored tunics were tossing wooden balls and suspending them in the air in defiance of nature's marvelous power. In response to the bells, the jugglers stuffed their balls into the voluminous pockets of their kirtles and betook their jingling caps around the corner of the church porch, vacating the performance space for the mystery play, which was the next act on the program.

The musicians—cheerily clad in jewel-toned cotehardies and hose, one leg sapphire-hued and the other the color of rubies, a fashion that was the height of sophistication and so contrary in character to that of the drama which was about to commence—began to play a merry tune upon their recorders, pipes, and mandolins, and to shiver their tambourines dripping with tiny tinkling bells and rainbows of fluttering ribbons. But then a player, garbed in a long black robe, walked onto the stage. The man's visage was covered with a hood, and both his hood and his robe were of black-dyed wool, block-printed with the white bones of a skeleton. So skillfully did the actor strut upon the boards that he gave a realistic impression of a walking corpse. The prattle of the citizenry dwindled to a subdued tittering. The actor gravely chanted:

"The Blessings of God Most High
Upon Their Most Holy Majesties the King and Queen, Our Sovereigns,

Upon Our Holy Father, the Pope, God's General on Earth,
And upon The Most Royal Duc and Duchesse,
Who Honor the People in this Place Gathered with their Most
    August Presence,
Who Most Graciously Condescend to Share in Our Humble Fes-
    tivities,
Know All that I am Death,
And Neither High nor Low may Refuse My Invitation."

A pall descended upon the audience, its merriment doused; even the ale lost its power to anaesthetize. In the fourteenth century, every facet of a person's daily life was punctuated by reminders that all ends in death. Had not God in His Great Mercy sent the Black Death to exhort His children to a proper humility, in charity to remind humankind of its lowly estate? In his conceit, man had vainly attempted to supersede the will of God by burning witches and exterminating felines, their familiars, thinking to halt the Pestilential Scourge, but Our Heavenly Father had had the last laugh, as fully half the people in the city had bled out their lives in the Plague, despite these awful measures. Death reached out his hand to a stylish Lady in a blue silk dress who was observing the performance from her litter. She paled.

"Thou canst not refuse my invitation to dance," Death breathed softly.

The Lady joined him upon the stage.

"The churl works hard from birth to death,
    Wears his skin to the bones,
    Ploughing the earth, Harvesting the Grain,
    He works until the Day of Death."

As he sang, the actor in the skeleton costume pointed his gloved hand, painted to suggest bones, in the direction of a peasant who, busily draining the last drops of ale from his wooden tankard, failed to remark his gesture. The man's neighbor tapped him on the shoulder, startling him, so that he spit the last draught from his mouth. The chosen man wiped his mouth with his sleeve and climbed the wooden steps to join Death upon the stage.

One soul at a time, Death selected people to join his *Danse Macabre:* a stable boy in rags, a cook in an apron, a knight with a painted shield on his tunic, a shepherd with a crook, an archer carrying an arrow and a king wearing a crown, an abbess in a wimple, a maiden in a veil, a pope in a white gown trimmed in gold paint and a high white headdress upon his brow, and a monk wearing a robe of brown stuff and open sandals, some of them people from the audience and some players belonging to his ensemble. To giddy drumming and tambourine-rhythms, the circle of dancers whom Death had assembled, alternating male and female, stepped in precise courtly footwork to the music, tracing patterns of increasing complexity, moving into and out of the circle in an intricate and pernicious choreography.

At the end of an hour of frenetic dancing, Death came forward once more.

> "I extend my Invitation Dread
> To the Most Royal Duc du *Joie de Vivre*
> To Danse the *Danse Macabre* with Me
> Who Reigns Eternally when Kings and Ducs are Dust."

Bowing low, he stretched his hand toward the royal personage.

Taken aback, the Duc hesitated, but he was urged forward by the looks of the Duchesse and his brother, as well as by his own sense of his dignity, which demanded that he exhibit no trepidation before his inferiors. As he approached the stage, the dancers, with much bowing and curtseying, made such obsequies as were due to their lord. Death himself descended the steps, knelt, and kissed the hand of the Duc, and then led him up the stairs to the platform.

"God on High (he sang) brings down the Mighty,
All to him are dust, Each to his own Estate on Earth
To Humbly Serve His Purpose,
Only Death Remains when His Will is Done."

Somberly, Death offered the Duc a golden goblet encrusted with glass cut to impersonate gems, and from it the Duc drank wine spiced with myrrh. When Death took back the cup from the Duc's hands, the musicians resumed their playing.

The ring of dancers stepped and hopped, twined insanely in and out, wove crisscrossed patterns on the floor, faster, ever faster, struggling to keep pace with the increasing tempo of the music. After thirty arduous minutes, Death separated himself from the perspiring circle of flesh and blood; and, lifting his hand, he signaled to the musicians to cease their playing.

"Cast Thy Bodies upon the Ground (he said),
Shrive Thy Souls, Grovel, for Thou Art Dust;
This is how the *Danse Macabre* Ends
At the Judgment Seat of God."

He pointed to the floor, whereupon the dancers lay themselves upon the wooden planks. Pope lay next to shepherd and knight stretched alongside cook on the dirty floor. Duc du Joie de Vivre was led to a tapestry-draped "throne," upon which he sat and then closed his eyes in a semblance of death, in obedience to the stage directions prompted by Death. The expansive plaza was silent as a tomb—for the audience was holding its breath in contemplation of the hideous scene, the *memento mori,* so like the bloodbath it had witnessed daily for the previous two years when the Plague had made its home in their city, and which had only recently ended. Even the wind ceased to blow.

Death exhorted the members of the congregation to think on their own deaths and the Judgment that awaited them on the Last Day; indeed, seldom was an opportunity missed to remind the flock that their earthly lot was hard labor and renunciation of good things.

Surreptitiously and *sans* ceremony, the Duchesse exited the spectator platform with the brother of the Duc and his retainers, driving off in the royal coach once their party was beyond the purview of the people in the plaza. Uncomfortable in the presence of Death, the good people in the crowd were contemplating their feet, avoiding both each other's eyes and the macabre tableau of the deceased upon the stage; thus they failed to take note of the silent departure of the nobility.

After a time, the people in the plaza began to shift their positions and to look furtively to their friends, wondering how long they were to remaining standing there without speaking, and when they had would have leave to depart.

At length a thirsty miller said to his wife that he was going to the tavern, for they had stood about doing nothing long enough; following his lead, everyone else began to disperse. The erstwhile dancers rose to their feet, looking for Death to receive their next commands of him, but Death was nowhere to be found.

In consternation, the Lady in blue wagged her golden tresses, which were artfully woven with pearls. She approached the Duc du Joie de Vivre (to protest their desertion by the Master of Revels)—and she found the Duc slumped over his throne, his eyes still closed. When her lord failed to respond to her entreaties, the Lady, oh so timidly, ventured to touch his royal person—whereupon he fell forward onto his face. The Lady screamed and fainted.

"Guard!" called the crowd. "Murder!"

The peasant who had been called to the danse retrieved the gold-colored goblet and held it to his nose.

"Poison!" he cried. "The Duc du Joie de Vivre has been poisoned!"

The audience became a mob as it began its pursuit of Death—some searching the cathedral, some the streets, alleys, and houses—only to find that he was gone, with his wagons and his troupe of actors.

"What has become of our Duchesse? And where is the new Duc, our dead Duc's brother?" the people cried in fear and sorrow.

Heedless of the souls amassed there, a squad of goodly knights mounted upon noble steeds galloped into the cathedral plaza, the ducal banner flapping from their lances, and the good Duc's subjects careened into one another in their haste to avoid being trampled by them. The Captain of the Guard proclaimed a warrant for the apprehension or death of Death, and a suitable reward, but none could identify the actor, for he had not given his Christian name nor had they seen his face without the skull-embellished hood.

On the third day following the funeral, the new Duc du Joie de Vivre wed his brother's distraught widow with much pomp and circumstance in the cathedral. An extravagant festival was planned in honor of their nuptials, with lavish feasting and spirits, as well as gifts of grain and gold coins, for all the people.

"*He's here!*" shrieked the lady in blue, who was standing in her place of honor behind the Duchesse at the banquet table. "Death! *Death is here!*"

The wedding guests turned to look at the door, at which the lady was pointing. Unsheathing their swords, the Duc's bodyguard bolted out the door and dispersed in the street in pursuit of the invader, for Death had disappeared!

When the guests turned to look at the table where the newly wed couple sat, they cried their mournful lamentations to heaven in one woeful voice.

The Duc and Duchesse du Joie de Vivre lay with their faces

in their plates, their dark red, clotting blood streaming from their ears and eyes onto the silver dinner service, taken by the Black Death to their final reward. It would only be a matter of hours before Death took them all.

In the Shadow of Castle Dracula

Katya sighed, dreading the approach of nightfall, aware that the daystar's quotidian descent into the underworld would displace the shades of Hades into the world of the living. As she closed the door of the hotel behind her, the sky was already burning purple, and the twilight overture of yelps and barks and howls pitched her mind into a fever. The howling, the hideous ululations that ever filled the nights, made sludge of the blood in her veins and stones of her muscles. She whirled around: was it a shadow she had seen at the edge of her vision, or a night creature? Crossing herself, she whispered a *Pater Noster* and an *Ave Maria*.

Her shift done at the Golden Krone Hotel, Katya hastened home to make dinner for her family, hurriedly looking over her shoulder at the high mountain crag where the blue flames smoldered as they did each night when darkness overcame the province. The inn was busier than usual these days: a few days ago an English gentleman had arrived to do business at Castle Dracula, making everyone nervous, and people came together each day at the hotel to share their fears. Katya was a widow: six months ago her husband had been found dead, bloodless, at the edge of the forest. When, by nightfall, he had not returned from hunting, Katya had rung the alarum bell, and the men of Bistritz had gone in search of her Jan. They found his corpse, his throat shredded by sharp teeth, and his terror evident in his still bulging, lifeless eyes. Katya had to wipe her eyes with her apron whenever she thought of him. She walked quickly, for she had four children at home: Anna, the eldest at eight, who watched over the little ones; Jan, who was six; Mara, four; and a poor babe, Peter, who had never known his father. They would be hungry, for she had worked late. It was dark, and the wolves were singing their elegiac melodies—and the hairs stood up on Katya's neck. She broke into a run. Something was wrong.

She flew down the cobbled street, the crucifix she always wore on a chain bouncing against her chest as her feet hit the stones, past numerous wooden doors bolted against the night and hung with garlic, to her own home in the row of adjoining houses in the narrow street. When she saw that the door of her house was open, swinging in the invisible breeze, she was scarcely able to move her legs or fill her lungs, for her heart was pounding so hard that its drubbing on her rib cage overwhelmed all her senses. They were dead! Her babies! Slaughtered!

She ran to Anna. Anna was lying on the floor before the hearth; her throat had been sliced from chin to navel, her torn flaxen dress soaked with blood. Jan—oh, God, Jan—her little Jan was slumped in a chair beside the table, his neck broken, and two puncture marks prominent in the cleft beneath his jaw. Mara lay in the fireplace, tossed into the ashes, her blood drained from her, too, by means of twin perforations in her throat. The babe—Peter—where was her babe? Katya looked in every corner, beneath the table and the bed they all shared, under the blankets. It was a small house, so it did not take her long. She went to the door and wailed into the desolate street. She saw it then—

A great black wolf was turning the corner, her babe in its jowls! Katya ran after it, her breath coming in desperate, laborious draughts. The powerful fiend was too swift. Katya had almost despaired of saving her child by the time she reached the stable of the dark and shuttered Golden Krone, yet she entered the equine hostel and led a cart horse from its stall, leapt upon its back, and set off in pursuit of the wolf. Katya prayed that it was not too late, as she kicked the horse's side to make it go faster—faster. The horse foamed at the mouth and its sides slickened with sweat as its hooves pounded the dirt road. Katya clung to the horse's neck and squeezed her knees into its ribs. The cold moonlight glimmered on the frost-covered grass on either side of the road. And the wolves howled all around her, causing the horse to shy. But Katya willed the horse to obey her: her will was too strong for the animal to resist—the life of her child was at stake!

The mountains drew nearer, their very height obstructing the moon, so that the wan beams of the night sky were diffused and dim now, making it difficult to see the road. Blue flames were visible, here and there, in the darkness. The sides of the mountains approached the road, now, high walls of rock to the left and to the right of Katya—the Borgo Pass! Fatigued and terrified, the distraught animal reared upon its hind legs, whinnying a frantic appeal, and throwing Katya from its back. She got up on her feet, felt her throbbing limbs to tell if they were broken, and watched the horse bolt in the direction from which they had come. Her crucifix lay on the ground, the chain broken in the fall.

She started running, panting, her spit dribbling from her mouth, up the steep incline of the Borgo Pass. She no longer felt her weariness, no longer felt her heart laboring to pump her legs with blood, no longer suffered the difficulty of filling her lungs with breaths, no longer possessed an awareness of anything but the necessity of reaching Peter in time. At length she came to the castle at the top of the mountain—the wolf! The wolf was running into the gate—and Peter was still in its jaws. *Please God in Heaven, her babe was still alive! Please Blessed Mother, please protect my babe!*

Katya ran through the towering iron gates creaking crooked-

ly on ancient hinges, into the courtyard of the black and malevolent castle, a hideous silhouette against the icy orb in the sky.
The clouds slipped by the front of the moon, causing the shadows in the courtyard to jump to and fro, as if they had living
agency. In the ashen light Katya saw the wolf enter the great
timber doors of the castle. She tried to reach the doors before
they closed—too late! They slammed shut just as she reached
them. She tried to pull them open—she pounded on the doors—
she cried,

"Give me my babe! My little Peter! For all that is sacred on
earth and in heaven, give me back my babe!"

Katya stood before the immense, barred egress of the ancient
edifice, sobbing and pleading and praying.

"Peter! Give me my Peter! He is only a poor, fatherless
babe!"

She slumped to the ground, weeping in a pitiful heap upon
the flagstones. When the sun came up, she was still there. She
looked up to the windows: there was a man looking down at her
from one of them.

"Oh, please, good sir, please help a poor mother. A wolf has
stolen my babe—"

Her petition was arrested by the ominous refrain of growling
disharmony from behind. She turned. A dozen snarling, snap-
ping great black wolves had come into the courtyard, barring the
gate. They advanced toward her deliberately, their thick black
coats ruffling in the chill wind and two rows of sharp teeth evident in each of their twelve opened maws.

"Blessed Virgin, God in Heaven, help me!"

Imprisoned in Castle Dracula, Jonathan heard Katya's an-
guished plea and looked out the window, where he watched the
wolves tear her into pieces and devour her. Although he was
High Church, he tearfully made the sign of the cross and prayed

to God and his Blessed Mother for the poor mother and that he might make it home alive to Mina. He knew that he must contrive his escape at once.

The Devil's Own

They were so large that they covered the sky—so great that they swallowed up the whole world—and their sable wings thrashed up perilous squalls, uprooting scores of centuries-old trees and then dropping them upon the thatched rooves of the woodsmen's cottages. Sheep and dairy cows took wing, tempest-propelled into the sky.

The schoolmaster bade us take shelter beneath our benches; and then, crossing himself and muttering his prayers in Latin, he lifted the Holy Bible from the desk. Raising the book over his head, he recited, "The Lord is my shepherd . . ." Radu and I clung to each other—each, in equal parts, terrified and loath to be seen as frightened. "I shall not want . . ."

The roof swept toward the gale-blackened sky, torn from our schoolhouse by immense claws. Splinters rained like arrows in the night. "Though I walk in the valley of the shadow of death . . ." His sentence unfinished, the great branch of a once-mighty oak tree pierced the breast of the schoolmaster, impaling him upon the floor of the one-room schoolroom (which was situated in the forest just beyond the castle walls) in a spreading pool of his own blood.

The frenetic shrieks of a howling chorus ascended to heaven as the smoke from a funeral pyre—schoolboys, the sons of my father's boyars, looking death in the face. I alone did not cry out. Instead, I looked up—boldly, as became the son of the Voivode—confronting the roofless prospect of the firmament. My eye caught the six eyes of a three-headed dragon that swooped down at me in a diabolical and grotesque arabesque. When it glided heavenward again, I found myself in its claws.

It bore me through the air. Beyond the clouds, I was able to almost touch the stars. I shouted "Huzzah!" for joy. I should have been chilled, flying so swiftly through the icy downpour, but I was much too pleased to pay heed to the storm—and I was nestled in the soft fur of the underbelly of the dragon. I looked down upon the flattened schoolhouse, drawing bravery from the possibility that I might have been the lone survivor, the victor. I knew that, henceforth, I would be invincible—that men would tremble before *me!* The great lizard carried me over the breadth of the kingdom, and I understood that it was all to be mine. This was my destiny: for I was Dracula, son of Dracul—the Dragon!

The dragon bore me high above the mountains, from which great height the rugged Carpathians looked as mere plow-combed furrows in a field of golden wheat. We followed the course of an ancient river, said to be curst, whose fetid waters twist insanely within the deep, rimmed bowl of a granite gorge, nourishing the murky basin of Lake Hermannstadt. At length we descended into a stony valley where no plants grow, a desert of sharp and jutting boulders. The great claws held me closer to the belly of the beast as the dragon skimmed the rocky floor, dove into a cave of adamant, and then glided through miles of unlighted labyrinthine tunnels into the depths of the mountain.

Although I was blind in the blackness of the chasm, my ears caught the murmuring of a subterranean watercourse. I felt cold and damp, and yet I was hot. I smelled sulfur. When the dragon came to a rest, myself still in its claws, I found that I was un-harmed. A light appeared—a crimson shaft—which, widening into a crimson beam, revealed the entrance to ap murky cavern. As a colossal door opened inward into the red glow, I perceived that it was graven with strange characters—written in an inhuman script that I had never seen before—depraved pictograms and unhallowed symbols.

A tall, red man appeared in the threshold. His skin, crusted with scales as if it had been scorched in the flames of Hades, reeked of damnation. His eyes, blacker than onyx, were soulless voids. From the elongated sleeves of his scarlet robe he stretched forth two skeletal hands toward me, indicating with ten bony digits, upon each of which I spied a ring worth an emperor's ransom, that I should approach. The dragon released its hold upon me, and I tumbled to the floor. In a moment I was upon my feet—as became a man who would command men.

"Wizard, why hast thou brought me here?" I demanded of the dark Lord of the grotto.

"Vlad Dracul, thou art chosen of the Devil for his Scholomance, called also the School of the Dragon, for thou art the scion of the House of Dracul, a dynasty that has long enjoyed the favor of the Prince of Darkness."

"Dark Lord, I humble myself before thy vast wisdom; for I am yet but an eager and apt scholar, desiring to partake of thy strange and fantastic knowledge—and to master the Powers of Darkness."

"Therefore, Prince Vlad, for seven years thou shalt abjure the light, learning everything there is to know about the race of men, in the Scholomance beneath the mountains. Thou shalt converse with the beasts that grovel on their bellies, as well as those of the creatures that scavenge in the seas. Thou shalt ride the great winged dragons to the far side of the moon and down into hell. Thou shalt know the secret of Attila the Hun. All the forbidden knowledge of nature, and that which is above nature, shall be thine."

*

Seven years passed, and I returned above ground to claim my father's throne. During my time below the earth my father had been murdered, one brother had been killed, and the other taken prisoner by the Infidels. In the absence of the Draculas, the boyars had overreached themselves. I soon remedied that: I forced the boyars, and their women and their children, to raise my new castle, high upon the precipice of Poenari. Of those who survived the arduous labor, I slew them all, many of them by driving the stake through their bodies. I would dine beneath the impaled traitors, watching them dance upon their lofty pikes and delighting in the music of their moans, as their warm blood filled my golden goblets.

My bloodlust would not be sated by mere savagery, however. I hunted each night, feasting upon the blood of my serfs, stalking them in the dark—in the form of a wolf or a bat, or even the wisps of a fog—rending their throats with my teeth—damning their souls! This was the secret of Attila the Hun, the invulnerability of the Undead. I was Undead now—immortal—the Suzerain of Darkness, devourer of souls.

Centuries passed. Half a thousand years. No one lived who dared to resist me, and my dominion was undisputed. Jaded, there came upon me a restlessness, a desire to venture forth into the world, to discover how it had altered since my matriculation in the Scholomance, to make new conquests. To this end I obtained recent almanacs and travel books, maps, weighty legal tomes, and newspapers from every nation.

I was intrigued by London. The capital city of England—a modern marvel with all the latest inventions, surpassing even the printing press. Queen of the world, Britannia holds the continents in her sway, and her streets are teeming with multitudes of people. The women in the newspapers, they are so beautiful, the Englishmen so noble.

I directed my secretary to reply to an advertisement, which I had seen in a London newspaper, for a solicitor, a Mr. Hawkins, with whom I corresponded over the course of several months regarding the acquisition of properties in England. The English I found adept in commerce and logistical matters, such as the best means of transporting boxes of my native soil across the Continent and the North Sea. Mr. Hawkins has agreed to send his assistant, Mr. Jonathan Harker, who will facilitate my dealings and with whom I can practice my English skills.

As Harker arrives today, I will bring this memoir to a close. Tomorrow I shall begin a new chapter, set in England. A fresh land to conquer. A new people to subdue. For I am Voivode.

Tales of Magic and Magical Beings

Stray Gods and Cats

She applied her brick-red lipstick quickly, taking care that it did not bleed beyond the borders of her full lips. She fumbled a bit with the lipstick case, as she closed the tube and placed it in her purse. She lifted her silver brush and fluffed energy into her long blonde hair. She hated it when it lay flat and lifeless, and she was glad that she had been born with a full coif. She glanced at the silver alarm clock on the vanity. It was time to leave. Her first lecture started in an hour. She stood, pushed the stool into the recess of the vanity, and reached for her briefcase. As she walked to the door, the slight edge of a frayed thought crept into her consciousness, and she pushed it aside as if it had been a stray hair. She tried to keep the darkness at bay. She opened the door and went out into the full light of the sun, toward the car in the driveway. She loved her life, she did.

Through her classes and faculty meetings she tried to focus on the present. Past and future, the abyss, always tried to encroach. She refused to look into the deep. Refused its dark allure. She nodded, and she smiled her beautiful white-toothed greeting at the students in the hall and the president of the university as he started for the stairs. She noted the extra seconds in which his gaze lingered, slightly longer than would be considered seemly, and she thrilled to the knowledge of her powers of attraction.

29

He waved, and she nodded back. He came toward her.

"Did you get my email? You're up for an award. Let's get together and discuss it over cocktails one evening this week."

She accepted the compliment with grace, having grown accustomed to honors, betraying no sign of complacency or anything akin to an attitude of superiority. Ease. That was it. She felt easy with herself, her life. It was crazy to think for a minute that it could fall apart. She stopped, pulled her foot back. It was her imagination: she had thought for a second that she might be about to step off the edge of a cliff.

The cell phone in her pink Dior bag started to sing, "Masquerade," from Weber's *Phantom of the Opera*. She let it go to voicemail and returned to her office. Shutting the door, she poured a glass of amontillado and drank it, standing, in one long draught. After replacing the glass next to the bottle on the bookshelf, she blotted the remaining drops from her red lips with a paper napkin and sat in the chair behind the large mahogany desk. She shuffled the folders in front of her and leafed through a stack of papers to grade. Eighteenth-Century Gothic Literature. What did her students know of terror and malevolent beings? She stifled the urge to sweep them off her desk. The phone began to serenade her again. She answered it. Malcolm. All right.

"Hello, sweet. Just grading papers. Ready to ditch this gig. Eight o'clock? Lovely."

She picked up her briefcase and exited the office. On the way to her car, she returned the smiles and the waves of a score of people who evinced pleasure at seeing her. She clenched her teeth behind her full red lips.

The dinner in the five-star restaurant was superb, as usual. The after-dinner lovemaking top-notch, as usual, too. After Malcolm went home, it was just Eleanor—and her thoughts. Eleanor, named by her romantic mother for Eleanor of Aquitaine, based on the Katherine Hepburn version of the willful queen who defied God and king for her right to hew her own destiny, and who never lost her wit and aplomb while doing it, despite the encroachment of the castle walls imprisoning her. Eleanor's mind, in its dusty corners, caught a glimpse of cold stone walls, slick with the damp of the tomb that was drooling down the crumbling mortar. She clamped the iron doors of her mind shut. I will not. Go there. She was tired. God, she needed her sleep. The crisp white sheets and the thick down comforter called to her. She said, "I'll sleep tonight," doubting it even as she spoke the words.

The next day was Saturday, and she stayed abed a little later than she did on school days, not quite rested. She had dozed in increments, more awake than asleep, her typical night. As the sun penetrated the windows, she left her bed and made for the kitchen. Black coffee and toast. A jog through the park. A shower. That's how her Saturdays began.

She showered in the marble master bath, looked at her perfectly proportioned body in the wall of gold-framed mirrors. Check. She donned a Versace sundress, picked up her bag and her keys. She drove to the art museum to lunch with Melanie and then attend a concert of Egyptian classical music. She wore her ankh pendant, just for effect, a souvenir of a sabbatical in Giza, where she had visited the pyramids with an archaeologist friend.

Anaesthetized by two bottles of Spanish wine, turmeric- and cinnamon-flavored fava beans with flat bread, and a harem-style concert of woodwinds and strange percussion instruments, Eleanor returned home, debating whether to take a nap or read a book in her paneled library. She pulled her convertible into the driveway and walked to the front door.

"Hi, kitty-cat," she said, as she bent to scratch the top of the head of the short-haired grey cat with black spots that was sitting on the stoop; she was thinking that the feline was striking a very Egyptian cat-pose. He followed her into the house.

"You don't look like a stray. You must belong to someone." She wondered what kind of cat it was, and looked up spotted cats on a search engine. "An Egyptian Mau. You must belong to someone." She called the humane society and let them know she had found the valuable cat, and then she stretched out on her bed, sleepy with wine. The cat curled up on the bed beside her.

Eleanor dreamed that she was making love with her demon lover, a deeply tanned man with a tightly toned physique and thick, wavy charcoal hair. Whenever he visited her in her dreams he always promised her all the good things of this world, if only she would spend the afterlife in the underworld with him. He knew all her sweet spots, all the places on her body where his caresses would make her quiver, and all the places in her mind where the touch of his words would render her pliant to his will. He told her that she would be queen in the darkness beyond the tomb. Eleanor strove always to wake at this point, to avoid giving the answer.

Eleanor opened her eyes and blinked in the orange rays of the sunset coming through her blinds. She remembered the cat and stretched her arm in the bed to feel for him. Her hand was taken up between two strong hands and raised to a pair of velvet lips, and Eleanor rolled over to see who was in her bed. A tall, swarthy man, wearing a pleated white linen skirt and white linen headdress that was encircled by a gold band in the form of a serpent—this man was kissing her hand. She tried to pull her arm away, intending to leap from the bed, but he held it in an unyielding grasp. He maintained his hold on her hand with one of his own, and with the other he encircled her waist and turned her toward him. He quieted her attempt at a scream—with his tender kiss—but he did not release his hold.

He raised her up and walked her forcibly to an elaborate rectangular box, decorated with ankhs and falcon-headed men,
boats and jackals, and Mau cats in Egyptian-cat poses. He lifted
her up, his lips still pressing her mouth shut, and laid her in the
coffin.

"This night, and eternity, you will join the household of Osiris in a chamber concealed beneath the golden sands, beneath the
pyramids of the kings," he sang in a strange melody in an arcane
language that Eleanor had never heard before, yet which she
somehow understood as she saw the lid of the coffin come down
between her and her life. "I have desired you ever since you
came to me in Egypt."

The Magic Crystal Ball

"I love it!" Sandy gushed. "Mommy! Daddy! Thank you!"

"Let's try it out," her father said. "Sandy, can you ask it if
we're going to win the lottery? I'd quit my job right this minute,
Barb, if I had advance notice."

"Sandy, Bill, let's sit down at the table. Here, take these dishes to the kitchen, please, Bill. I'll move the birthday cake out of
the way. Then you can tell us our fortunes, Sandy."

Having cleared away the detritus of Sandy's eighth birthday
celebration, the Fields gathered around the table for a demon-
stration of her favorite gift, a Magic Crystal Ball. Ever since she
had seen a television commercial for the popular toy, Sandy had
been begging for one. She was always reading books about
witches, ghosts, and vampires—and she was a good reader, too,
reading three years above her age cohort. A *Hocus Pocus* DVD
was among her birthday treasures (the whole family usually
watched scary movies together on Saturday nights). Finding the
Magic Crystal Ball for their daughter had been a challenge,
though, for the toy was very popular that spring and the toy

stores all had them on back order. Bill was diligent, though, and he had located one in an esoteric shop in another town, a shop that specialized in wares such as crystals and incense.

"Daddy, come on!" Sandy called to her father, who was still in the kitchen.

When they were all seated, Sandy asked the Magic Crystal Ball if they would win the lottery. She turned the ball over, and the answer showed in white letters glowing out of inky fluid, through the window on the bottom of the ball:

"The stars say no."

"I guess I'd better go to work tomorrow, then," sighed Bill.

"Let me ask next!" cried Sandy. "Magic Crystal Ball, will I be lucky?"

"Probably," was the answer that floated up when she inverted the ball.

"Silly, you didn't ask whether you would have good luck or bad luck," her mother teased, patting her daughter on the head.

Sandy asked the ball questions all night until it was time for bed, and when she was tucked in for the night her ball was on the table next to her bed. In the morning she was up with the sun, asking the ball more questions. When her mother came to rouse her for school, she found Sandy already awake and seated at her desk, writing down all the answers contained by the floating die inside the ball:

"You can count on it."

"The odds are in your favor."

"Vibrations are mixed."

"The stars say no."

"Outlook positive."

and so forth.

Barb had to be a little stern to discourage her daughter from taking the Magic Crystal Ball to school; and, when Sandy was back home after school, Barb had to coax her out of her room—where she was asking yet more questions of the ball—to eat her dinner.

The next day Barb received a call from Sandy's teacher, Mrs. Markham, who told her that the girl had one of her classmates in tears. Sandy had brought the Magic Crystal Ball to school and, on the playground, she was telling the other children that she had magic powers and could see into the future. A boy named Arnold asked her whether his sick mother would get better, and Sandy turned the ball over and told him the answer of the Magic Crystal Ball:

"The stars say no."

The youngster was so distraught that the principal had to call his parents to take him home.

Sandy's parents gave her a good talking-to, explaining that it was wrong to frighten other people with her toy; they made it clear that she was not to bring it to school anymore.

Although there were no further occurrences of a concerning nature, Bill and Barb noticed that Sandy was becoming more withdrawn, playing alone in her room more than outdoors or with her neighborhood friends, as she had done before, and she seemed less exuberant when eating her favorite foods or watching monster flicks on the weekends. They decided not to give undue weight to what was, most likely, a temporary phase, such as all children must experience as part of their development; instead, they bought her a telescope and a skateboard, attempting to broaden her interests.

One night, when it was quite late and her parents had gone to sleep, Sandy was sitting up beneath her sheets, plying her Magic Crystal Ball with questions and reading its answers with a flashlight. Although she had never heard the word, she was feeling all the power of an oracle: not only could she foretell future events, but she could influence people by sharing or withholding the prophecies of her ball. She turned the ball once—twice—*a third time!* She scrambled from her bed to the desk to consult her list. *It was not there*—of course, it was not. And yet, when she looked a fourth time the scrying ball yielded the same command:

"Steal a candy bar."

Frightened, Sandy almost ran to her parents' room—almost jumped into bed with them. But she did not stir, for she knew that they would be dismayed to learn that she had been up half the night, entreating answers of her Magic Crystal Ball; and she knew that they would be unhappy to see her so afraid. Not wanting her parents to deprive her of her enthralling new prognostication device, Sandy stayed put in her own bed. She hardly slept a wink, though.

The next morning, when she went to the market with her mother to pick up something for dinner, she slipped a Milky Way into the pocket of her jacket while her mother was paying for the groceries. She had never done that before. She had never even thought of stealing before. She was not even all that fond of candy bars.

This was how Sandy began leading a double life. Now that she had her first secret—which she had to keep from her parents—she learned to dissemble. She put some effort into acting like her old self, in order to deflect her mom and dad from inquiring into her new fads, new phases. Sandy felt alternately mortified with herself and proud of her newfound skills and independence. At school she asked the librarian to show her books about fortune-telling, and she added the terms "psychic" and "clairvoyant" to her burgeoning vocabulary.

On her ninth birthday she received a Birthday Barbie in a pink tulle dress and a boxed set of Louisa May Alcott books. She was very happy with her gifts and her pink cake; yet she was thinking of the Magic Crystal Ball awaiting her in her bedroom. Later that night, when she was supposed to have been asleep, she brought the plastic ball into her bed with a flashlight, pulled a blanket over her head, and turned the sphere over to scry her fortune.

"Make a crank call."

Sandy leapt out of bed, and the ball hit the hardwood floor with a clunk. By the time her father knocked on her door and opened it to see if everything was all right, she was back in bed, feigning sleep. Now Sandy was a smart girl, and, though she could not have explained what she felt intuitively, she knew that something was not quite right.

The next afternoon, when her father was playing golf and her mother was reading a book, Sandy dialed the Sandersons' phone and told Mrs. Sanderson that her daughter, Jean, had drowned in the pool at the recreation center. Barb came running out of the study, her book in her hand, when she heard the heart-wrenching screams coming from the house next door.

"Sandy, stay right here. I'm running over to check on Linda."

Ten minutes later Barb returned. The Sanderson girl had been riding her bicycle around the block and had been nowhere near the recreation center.

"What a cruel thing to do," she told Sandy. "Some crank nearly broke Linda's heart."

Sandy experienced a strange admixture of sympathy for their neighbor and . . . glee—glee at having gotten away with something so daring.

The residue of the summer was spent in bicycling, swimming, picnicking, and visiting the fairs. Sandy read all the Alcott books and a few more. Little of note occurred. Whenever Sandy inverted her Magic Crystal Ball, which she did often, she received the conventional responses:

"You can count on it."

"The odds are in your favor."

"Vibrations are mixed."

"The stars say no."

"Outlook positive."

and so on.

One day, as she was sitting on the floor, arranging her marbles into a circle, into the center of which she placed her Birthday Barbie, she thought to look at her Magic Crystal Ball. She got up and went to her desk, picked up the ball, and returned to her circle of polished stones. Sitting cross-legged on the floor, she rolled the Magic Crystal Ball in her palms and turned it over to read its message.

"Burn the school."

"No!" Sandy cried, hurling the ball from her. It rolled noisily across the narrow planks and collided with the baseboard. A small fissure appeared in the plastic.

Bill noticed the Magic Crystal Ball in the trash the next morning, and he mentioned it to his wife. At breakfast he asked Sandy why she was throwing out the Crystal Ball.

"I'm just tired of it, Daddy. Maybe I'm getting too big for toys," was her reply.

Barb rescued the ball from the trash and placed it in a box of items she was collecting for the rummage sale to benefit the PTA. Over the weekend she dropped the box off at the school. The gym was a hectic place, filled with volunteers accepting donations carted in bags and boxes by dozens of families. Folding tables were being arranged around the perimeter of the spacious room, and signs were being carried out the door to be placed along the street.

"Looks like a storm is coming in," Margie Dickerson said to Barb. "I hope it blows over. We've had way too much rain lately."

"They'd better hurry and bring their things in, so they don't get soaked before the sale," Barb answered. "The money raised is going to purchase gym equipment, isn't it?"

The lights flickered, causing the two women to pause in their conversation.

"I hope we're not going to lose power," Margie said, glancing frequently at the upper-level windows. "Oh, no—hear that? It's a downpour! I'm not leaving until it lets up: I've just had my hair done."

Out on the road, a fuel truck failed to negotiate a curve in the deluge, for lack of visibility. It lost its traction, flipped onto its side, and slid into the gymnasium entrance of the school, where it burst into flames. No one who was present in the gym at the time survived.

To Necrophilia

O rosy Dawn, ye bright blush of heaven's
Angels who behold my loveliest paradise—
Celestial spirits are envious even
Of my Necrophilia's emerald eyes.

Living maiden, thy glance is sorcery,
Enchants, captivates, ensnares, enslaves
Mortal man in thrall to thy mystery,
Conqueror conquered, lord reduced to knave.

No power hath my cold love's sparkling jewels
In her soft, smooth, still alabaster brow
To influence, dictate, direct, nor fool
Her lord to thrall of bride—deceased now.

Ne'ermore shall wield such sweet sorceress glances,
Pallid marble stirs this poet's senses.

Lila in Arcadia

Lila exhaled, sank back into the velveteen upholstery of her seat in First Class, and gazed out the picture windows that lined both sides of the coach. Even with her nose pressed up against the glass, she had not been able to catch a glimpse of anything on either side of the rail car but trees. So many trees—immense trees—dusky shades of towering conifers and leafy, deciduous trees, whizzing by the windows of the train. Under other conditions, she might have indulged in speculation regarding the botanic taxonomies of the gargantuan flora in the ancient forest through which she was traveling. She might have attempted to guess the genus of this one, the species of that, for she was of a curious and bookish nature; instead, she was questioning the strange apprehension she felt when she peered into the inscrutable darkness outside the Amtrak coach, which was carrying her to Arcadia National Park, where she would be spending her vacation. She had booked a cabin in the woods—a small hut nestled among all those trees—which were visible now as only tall, ebony silhouettes in the lowering gloom. The travel agency's literature had promised a cascading river and a fine restaurant at the park lodge, both of which were located within walking distance of her secluded cabin. She had been saving for this trip all year.

The vast vegetative hulks of centuries-old firs flew past the windows; and these trees were of such prodigious numbers—and of such great height—that they barred nearly all the sunlight from the forest. Although it was still morning by her watch, only a thin row of plate glass windows divided her from the nearly total vernal darkness of the forest. *Undoubtedly, Maine does have a lot of trees,* Lila thought, *for which reason this region is generally regarded as beautiful, beckoning to enthusiasts of the natural, such as myself—and yet this primeval timberland route to Arcadia through which I am traveling is so densely packed with vegetation that it is scarcely penetrable by the light of day—and that is a tad creepy.* (Lila usually thought in formal language, verging on the poetic, for she had a lofty and adventurous soul.) Her skin was becoming goose-pimply, for she sensed, not only a poetic, but also a diabolical quality in the gloom that entombed the train: the gloom without the windows was so profound that it seemed to Lila to be a physical thing through which she traveled.

She rose and crossed the aisle to look out of the window on the other side of the car—and noticed that she was alone. Had the other passengers disembarked at a station, unnoticed by her because she had been engrossed in her book? Or had she just dozed off before the others had left the train? Thirteen fellow passengers had boarded with her only three hours earlier. She had spoken to none of them, opening her book straightaway, as soon as she had settled into her seat, as was her custom. She had, without raising her eyes from the page, merely nodded to the conductor as he had punched her ticket. Still, she had counted thirteen passengers ahead of her in line as she had climbed the grated metal steps and passed through the narrow doorway of the railway car, all of them wearing similar black hooded cloaks with silver symbols and none of them speaking. Lila wondered if the conductor would be returning to her car, or if he had done his duty in checking their tickets and was now settled somewhere comfortable for the duration of the journey. She looked out the window again: all she could see was a stygian opacity, and her own face reflected in the glass. She checked her watch—it was noon—and she marveled that the trees could grow so very thick that they obliterated all the light. The gloom was, in fact, so thick that the tracks on which she was riding seemed to be walled in by a tunnel, instead of laid out through a wood.

Lila was anxious now and decided to look in the next car, to ask the people there about the strange darkness of the eldritch forest. Holding onto the seats in the swaying car as she walked, she traversed the narrow aisle to the door at its terminus. She opened the heavy door and walked through the rocking passageway, and then she opened the door of the connecting compartment into the next coach. That car was empty, too!

Frightened, her breaths were coming rapidly now, as Lila hurried through the deserted car and flung open the door at the far end of it, letting in the clack-clack-clack of the wheels, and then passed through the connecting compartment and into the next car. There was not a soul in it!

She hurried on to the third car, and then the fourth, and then the fifth—she went through twelve of them, until she reached the thirteenth car. There was no one on board the train save herself! Gripping the woven fabric of the Standard-Fare seats that lined both sides of the aisle, she ran back through the cars, one by one, hastening back to her First-Class coach. Her book was still lying opened on her seat; beside it was the brochure from Putnam Travel, which she had tucked into the book, using it to mark her page; the cover of the pamphlet promised, mockingly, that a trip to the wild forests of Maine would open up new worlds for adventurous souls.

The desperate drubbing of her heart caused her knife-sharp pain, and Lila had a hard time breathing because of the tightness in her chest. She ran through the rolling First-Class car to its far end, went out the door, passed through the compartment. There was no car on the other side of her coach, only an iron railing where the door opened into the inky gulf outside the car. There was no locomotive, either—and there was no one aboard the moving train but herself!

As usually happens to most of us in a crisis, Lila had need of the ladies' room, and she squeezed herself into the miniscule, and somewhat purgatorial, cubicle and quickly did what she needed to do—while holding onto the handrails to prevent being her body being flung to the floor, as if she were inside a macabre carnival ride instead of a restroom. When she was done, she started back to her seat, clinging to the backs of the chairs, as the train rocked crazily to and fro. It seemed to be going faster now—and the clackety-clack sound of the wheels had a higher pitch, a more tympanic sound, as of iron wheels on a wooden trestle. She had better fasten her seatbelt.

She attempted to slide into the relative safety of her seat, but the floor went out from under her feet, causing her body to float in space. And then, with a loud cracking and splitting noise, the train plunged headlong into the blackness—blackness that was now not only to the left and right outside the windows, but all around the train, above and below it, a nocturnal abyss. Her body lifted from the floor by the centrifugal effects of the free fall, Lila screamed—inwardly only, for she was unable to produce a sound from her oppressed organs of vocalization.

She thought that she would die momentarily at the bottom of a great chasm, her body destined to become merely a spatter upon a barren ground. As the train hurtled toward what must become her tomb, the cars began to disintegrate: the metal exoskeleton liquefying and evaporating, the interior furniture dissolving. Lila found herself suspended in the hideous aether—a sightless and soundless, and a loathsome, netherworld.

As she drifted in the phantasmagoric void, her eyes began to adjust to the absence of light, and she could discern vague shapes at the bottom. There must be a bottom to it, for she could make out spires and steeples, pillars and labyrinths—the fantastic architectural elements of fairy realms and archaic romances. As she floated lower, Lila saw the twisted trees—trees shaped like pretzels or ampersands or even treble clefs. There were grottoes by lakes that plunged at oblique angles into the ground and then resurfaced, spraying jets like those that whales spurt from their blowholes, and from which silver rivers flowed up steep, amethyst hills.

As she fell even lower, she could see strange glyphs on the capitols of the lofty edifices; unseen figures garbed in black cloaks with silver ornaments, moving toward Cyclopean sphinxes in the distance; and slithering slimy toad-like creatures following in their wake. Ghastly creatures whose bodies were shaped like the bows of violins and whose frazzled purple hair dragged on the ground followed next in the hideous procession. And when she hit the ground with a thump, she found herself prostrate among a throng of grisly gnomes, whose red eyes stared at her from under their stupendous red brows, and whose fiery red faces implied a grim sort of welcoming for an uninvited guest. They blew their horns at her, and the macabre procession came to a halt.

The violin-bow-shaped creatures with the frazzled purple hair turned to face the musicians—and they parted, to make way for the slimy-toad-like things, who slithered over the crystalline ground to face the horn-blowers. The figures hidden by their black robes with the silver ornamentation turned next and walked back, toward Lila, who was sitting up now, on the crystalline ground, trying to fathom what had become of her.

She could not help noticing that the sky was an unrelieved blackness, and that the light by which she could see was emanating from the crystalline ground. The red-bearded and -browed gnomes crowded around her, hissing and blowing their horns, not looking pleased. The violin-bow-shaped creatures craned their necks to look over the gnomes, who were shorter than they, appearing mystified by what they saw on the crystalline ground. The black-garbed figures approached Lila, the toady-things slithering between what Lila supposed were their legs, concealed beneath their flowing robes.

"How came you here, girl?" asked one of the black-garbed figures, the one with the most silver ornaments.

"The train—it derailed and fell through the sky—and I landed here! I don't know how—I don't know where I am."

"You were on the train? *Our train?*" another black figure asked, the one with the second-most silver ornaments.

"I didn't know it was your train," Lila replied, in a daze, and in a state of suspended disbelief in the fantastic. "I must have gotten on the wrong train. The Putnam Travel Agency booked it for me."

"Putnam, you say," said one of the toady-things.

"Putnam," repeated all the red gnomes, becoming even redder.

"That explains everything," said the black-garbed figure who had the most silver ornaments. "The Putnams have, since the dawn of time, been trying to discover our secrets. They are a wicked clan, and we will not yield our knowledge to their kind."

"They keep trying, though," said one of the toady-things.

"Are you one of them?" asked a violin-bow-shaped creature, with frizzy purple hair.

"No, I am simply a customer who booked a vacation to Arcadia National Park through their travel agency. If only I had known," Lila sighed. "Would these, perchance, be the very same Putnams who orchestrated the witch trials in Salem? Some have called Ann Putnam 'America's First Bitch'—please pardon my language, I don't usually use such colorful words," she added, in a run-on sentence that betrayed her embarrassment.

"Yes, the same who called up the Powers of Darkness and laid the blame for the resulting inferno upon their innocent neighbors," a black-cloaked entity explained. "They have been trying to break through to Arcadia and steal our magic."

"You do have a beautiful city, and I apologize for trespassing, albeit quite unwillingly," replied Lila.

"I am afraid that we shall have to return you to your own world," the reddest gnome with the bushiest red beard said, with regret in his voice. "We are very glad to have met you, and we shall remember you fondly, although we cannot permit you to remember us, for we treasure our seclusion from the battles of outside worlds and dimensions."

"I thank you all from the bottom of my heart for your generous concern for my well-being," Lila responded earnestly; "yet I truly wish that I could enjoy an enduring relationship with you, for I hate to part, having only just made your acquaintance."

"Alas, dear Lila, that cannot be, because the risks to the safety of our world would be too great. As our parting gift to our new friend, however, we shall encourage you to visit us always, in your imagination. Yours is a poetic and an adventurous spirit: you shall therefore become a celebrated author, and your stories will be based upon your recollections of your visit to Arcadia, only you will think that your memories are the goods of your imagination. In this way we can be together always, yet preserve our distinct paths in the infinitude of possibilities. In this way we can still cherish our esteem for each other and be thankful for having met," the black-cloaked figure with the most silver ornamentation said. "Shall we embrace, to seal our pact, dear Lila?"

Lila threw her arms around the cloaked figure and, though she hugged it with all her might, she could not tell its shape beneath the black folds of its cloak. The black-cloaked figure hugged her back and whispered farewell into her ear. Silver sparkles and amethyst sprinkles filled the air, and Lila found herself, not in Arcadia, but on a train between Boston and Bangor, on her way to Arcadia National Park.

Yawning, she closed her book and removed a brochure from

between its pages—a booklet from Shangri-La Travel, which described the delights of her vacation destination. As she flipped through its pages, she conceived of a premise for the novel she hoped to begin writing on her vacation, and she began jotting notes in the margins.

The Color of Magic

She had always loved colors. Some shades of blue sent her into ecstasy. Some greens she found hideous, like those sickly greyish-greens you see in the hospital wards in old films; others, such as emerald-green jewel tones, made her feel regal and splendorous, while aqua greens sent her floating in waves of pure femininity, especially when combined with pinks à la Fragonard. Blue, though, oh all those blues—these were her favorites. Cornflower blue—she had to take deep breaths, for even thinking about the color set her to sighing. A glimpse of Delft blue was a beatific experience.

The trouble was that she had seen all the colors. She was simply sated with the same old spectrum, for she appreciated innovation and novelty, freshness and creativity. Oh, yes, you could recombine colors or use different hues. You could blend them, too, but the resulting shades were only more colors that were on the same old spectrum.

She yearned for more colors. She fantasized that there were additional colors somewhere else—some other planet, some other dimension. Perhaps, she thought, the want of new colors was the fault of our limited senses; and maybe appliances (like reading glasses and hearing aids) could enhance our ability to see new colors.

Her dreams had lately become variations on the theme of seeing herself climbing rainbows, flying over them, or walking beneath them. The rainbows would dissolve, however, when she reached them. She would run, panting, crying for mercy. But the rainbows would leave her lonely, bereft, unfulfilled. She would wake up in a cold sweat.

Clarice was roused from her reverie by the light notes of the door chimes. Annoyed at the interruption of her contemplation, she rose from her chair to answer the summons. The chimes warbled again just as she reached the door, and she turned the knob, saying, "Yes?" at the same time. She said no more, though. Instead, she closed her mouth and stared at the person enveloped in layer upon layer of fabrics: multiple skirts on top of skirts, blouse, vest, and scarves incalculable. Silks, rougher weaves, cottons, and woolens. Scarlet and gold and sapphire blue and black, yellow and neon pink; and one color she had never seen before—the gem in the woman's ring.

"What is that?" she asked the . . . woman (she was not sure of the person's gender, its form being so wrapped). "That color?"

"It is the color of magic."

"Magic, old woman—please explain."

"Invite me in and I will," said the gypsy.

"Very well, come in and tell me."

Clarice showed the gypsy into her house and said, "You are in. Now, tell me, please."

"I must sit."

"Please, sit here. Now tell me."

"I must have water and wine, for I am thirsty."

Clarice went to the kitchen and brought the gypsy a glass of each. She placed them on the end table. "Now tell me, please."

The gypsy drank the glass of wine. And then she drank the glass of water. Clarice sat in a chair opposite the old woman, trying to control her impatience.

"Old woman, please tell me about the color of magic."

"If you would see the color of magic, it is necessary for you to look closely at my ring. Come here, child."

Clarice stood up and walked over to the woman.

"You must kneel down, so that you can see better the color of magic."

Clarice knelt before the woman. The gypsy stretched out her hand.

"Take my hand in yours, girl."

Clarice took the gnarled hand into her own, feeling herself falling into the colors swirling inside the gem.

"What color is this? It is beautiful. It is joy," she breathed.

"Look deeply, girl. Enter into the bliss. Breathe the color of magic, feel it, and hear it."

"Oh, gypsy, it is divine."

"Deep, my child, gaze deep into the color."

"I have never felt such sublimity. I am lost in the beauty. I shall never want to look away."

"Gaze deeply. Allow yourself to enter the color, to feel it swirling around you."

"Gypsy, what is it? I am surrounded by beauty, but there is a hard dome above me. I am drowning in bliss, but there is clear ceiling over me. Gypsy, I cannot get out. Gypsy! What has happened?"

The gypsy admired the new cameo ring on her gnarled, bent finger. It was the profile of a beautiful woman. *What was her name?* she muttered to herself. *I forgot to ask her, and now I shall never know.* She put her gloves on and went out the door.

Strange Places

Haunted House

The dark night is electric. Moonless, starless, overcast, the sky hangs heavily over Felix Street like a pelt of thick sable, stifling the air, preventing a breeze. Behind quadrangular green lawns, old gingerbread houses with long, yellow-lit eyes pensively regard the strange people milling on the street and compare the Jack-o'-Lanterns on their own porches with those of the houses across the street and deem their neighbors' decorations lacking. The dogs of the street are excited, pulling at their leashes, trying to dig tunnels under chain-link fences, while the cats stay in the shadows or watch from windows and porches. The children babble nonsensically, upset candy bowls and orange paper cups of apple cider, awkward in their cumbrous Halloween costumes and sensing something weird in the air. Adults man their stations on painted plank porches, armed with candy and glow-wands, thinking at least this is only once a year, it's too bizarre to live like this every day. The man whose house stands on the corner of Felix and Grant waves cars onto his lawn with his flashlight and takes five dollars from the driver of each vehicle to park there, because the street is closed to parking and the haunted house at the end of the winding street has to be walked to.

Cars bouncing to loud music roll tires onto the grass, spill out of its doors cigarette and that other kind of smoke and twos and fours of high school and college kids after thrills. Where's the haunted house, they ask the homeowner, excited already, we want more, creeps and thrills, frights. Things jumping out at you making the girls scream so they hold onto you and who knows where that will lead. This night's electric they say.

Putting away his billfold, the man points down the street. It's a dead end, the haunted house is at the end, have fun. See where the streetlamp is going off and on, flickering like it needs a new bulb, the end of the dead end is around the bend by the street-lamp.

The kids say thanks man and put their arms around their boyfriends/girlfriends, pull out cigarettes and hip flasks, walk down the street. I like haunted houses they say, look at all the cute kids. I used to dress up as a werewolf, I was Superman. My mom was religious and wouldn't let us go trick-or-treating. Look at the Jack-o'-Lanterns, I like pumpkin pie. This is sup-posed to be the best haunted house in town, everyone's talking about it, vampires ghosts mad scientists. Don't let go of my hand, swear you won't, or I won't go in. I'll hold your hand.

How far is the haunted house? Oh, there, I see the street turn-ing—the old guy said it was around the bend. Trick-or-treating must be over, I don't see any more kids around. Except for the Jack-o'-Lanterns, the houses are all dark. Only the orange eyes, noses, mouths glow in the dark. Did everyone go to bed early?

Even the streetlights are dimmer. Down there—at the end of the street is the flickering one—the man said the house was down there. We're getting closer: see, you can see it now, the old Victorian house—all the windows all lit up! The only lighted house on the street.

Hey, where'd everyone go? Joe, Sandy? Did they find a par-ty, didn't say goodbye, will have to find their own way home. I didn't realize we were out so late, we're the only ones, Barb. At least it doesn't look closed, the house is all lit up. Don't be a scaredycat, Barb, that's why we're here.

Look—there's a graveyard, a little cemetery with a wrought-iron fence. How cool! It's the right night for a cemetery. Do you think it belongs to the people who own the house? The haunted house? See all the mist, the fog, coming out of the ground there, where people are buried six feet under? Bill, did you know that they bury coffins on top of each other, not one per grave? I learned that on a field trip to Sleepy Hollow. The lights are flickering. There's no moon or stars, only Jack-o'-Lanterns, and it's kind of spooky.

Hey, we're here. Let's knock on the door, use the big brass knocker.

"Good evening. It's very late. How can I help you?" the grey-haired woman in the purple dress asks when she opens the paneled front door with the frosted windows. Oh, yes, this is a haunted house, but not the kind that you're thinking of. Would you like to come in, look at it? I can offer you cider and doughnuts. You might as well look at the house, since you came all this way to see it. Oh, yes, that's my cat, Trolly, she and Dolly keep me company, they're spoiled.

This is the parlour—my grandfather was laid out there in his casket—see his funeral wreath in the glass box on the wall, flowers would probably crumble if you touched them now. This is the dining room: I always used to get the feeling that someone was there looking at me. I'll let you look around the upstairs, my knees are weak, be sure you go up to the third floor, the attic, it's full of fun old things, antiques. Oh, don't worry, take your time, I'll wait till you get back.

The house is weird, the lady's not right I don't think but harmless probably lonely. This is a long hallway, look at all the doors. Open one, a bedroom, another and a bathroom they had big families when it was built. Sad to be so empty now. Let's look in the attic real quick and then go. I'd really like to get out of here now there little stairs in the corner, must lead to the attic, trap door in the ceiling, pull on the rope it's opening.

There's the lightswitch, watch your head. What's with the electricity tonight streetlights flickering, houses dark but this one, and now very dim light from the bare bulb hanging from the ceiling. Let me try screwing it in tighter make it a little brighter.

Oh God what is that, the roof is open, purple light coming from the sky, but it is dark out, black not purple sky. Oh no let's go—where's the trap door and the stairs—they can't be gone we just can't see them, let's look.

There is no door no stairs. The room glows purple. The roof is gone, floors, walls too. Nothing but purple light. What are those things—they're coming at us. Yellow, walking on two feet with pointed noses and chins—great big mouths and sharp teeth. Help! Get us out of here! Somebody Help! LADY, HELP! SOMEBODY HELP!

Morning comes a school day, monsters of last night dressed in school clothes, shame the electricity was on the fritz last night Halloween ended too early at least the kids got their trick-or-treating in before the power went out. The man who lives on Felix and Grant wonders when they're coming for the last car left on his lawn or if he'll have to call the police later to get it towed.

Snowed In

Springtime in the Rockies. Hmph. A foot of snow coming down, beautiful view of Ponderosa pines on tall mountains, glopped with snow. A veil of flakes falling beyond the lacy curtains on my many-paned window. But the forecast had been for seventy degrees and sunshine, and I had packed shorts and T-shirts and cute summer dresses, and the heat had gone out in the old (or was that historic?) hotel. So I was looking at the ~~spring~~

winter wonderland out the window, wrapped in two blankets. I tried to order a hot toddy from room service, but the phone in my room did not work. I brewed a cup of coffee in the coffee maker on the dresser, opened my well-read copy of Radcliffe's *The Italian,* and fell asleep reading it.

When I opened my eyes, I stretched languidly in my uncomfortable chair, and then I saw a very large orange tiger cat in the doorway of my bathroom. I glanced at the door to the hall and saw that it was shut, and I looked back at the cat, wondering how she had gotten in. She was grooming her face, the way cats do, with the back of her paw, all softness and cuddliness and sheathed claws. I leaned over to retrieve a blanket that had slid to the floor, and when I straightened up I looked for the cat. She was not there. I called, "Hey, kitty," softly, and I got up to look for her in the bathroom. No sign. I turned and looked about the room. No trace of the kitty. I drew my blankets tight, sought my purse and my room key, and went downstairs to the dining room to get some dinner.

The eggplant cutlet was very good, but it did not stay hot very long in the heatless environment. The Irish coffee stayed warm long enough for me to warm my hands on it. I strayed to the gift shop, where I was able to purchase overpriced warm-up pants and a Rocky Mountain sweatshirt, which were a big help. I'd probably have to sleep in them. I walked through the great front doors onto the massive verandah and, seeing that the snow was rapidly accumulating, I returned inside.

I began to explore the aged hotel. I walked the narrow halls, long lines of closed white doors. At the end of each corridor the tall windows testified to the last stand of a desperate winter, which was hanging on for all it was worth. Occasionally a mirror appeared in a nook, pointlessly, placed too high to see yourself in, and the corridors were too narrow to allow for standing back to get a good look. A tiny staircase on the top floor led to a ceiling, or rather a trap door nailed shut in the ceiling: the stair was roped off.

I descended to the main floor, where the restaurant was still doing a good business, and explored the august lobby, whose well-worn paisley-patterned burgundy carpet and dusty end tables spoke wordless volumes about the appetite of time. I saw a darkened doorway at the far end of the room. The orange cat was disappearing into the gloom of the chamber beyond it. I followed.

I paused in the threshold and felt the wall for a light switch. Finding none, I stepped cautiously into the room. I called, "Hey, kitty," but received no reply. A ghostly luminescence through the window, created by the albino moonlight seeping through the mantle of snow, made shadows dance in the dark. I made out a long bar, in the reflected moonlight slung upon it by the mirrored wall behind it. A shadow reached for a bottle, one of many lined up along the mirrored wall.

"Hi," I said, "just looking around." The shadow answered not. I said, "Well, I guess I'll be going," and I turned to leave, almost stumbling over the orange cat, who galloped before me out of my way and through the door. Hastily following the feline, I emerged into the gaslit lobby.

Gaslit! Of course not, I thought, those globes must hold retro-looking bulbs. Being snowed in in an old hotel in the mountains certainly can play some tricks on a person's mind, I reasoned. It must be getting late, I don't see anyone else, the restaurant is closed.

Too wound up to consider sleep, I took the ornate brass lift to the lower level. The coffee shop was closed, the pastry cases devoid of temptation. I walked down the hall to a wooden door that was propped open and was labeled "The Tunnel."

The orange cat was sitting there, looking at me, twitching the tip of her tail. She called, "Mrowrr," and I went toward her. As I bent to pet her, she leapt away and sat again, looking at me, six feet further into the tunnel. Bare electric bulbs were suspended at intervals from the ceiling.

The tunnel was carved out of the mountain rock, and the hotel was built upon it. The passage seemed to wend indefinitely; even an occasional vertical tunnel pushed up into the rock or plunged down. The cat vanished silently into the ebony void, appearing once again at the edge of a black hole in the floor.

I crept toward the cat and the pit, intending to peer into the abyss if I could, and was stopped by the soft sound of a whimper. A keen of despair followed, and then a sob.

I drew back. The mournful sounds were succeeded by low moans. Immobilized by fear, it was all I could do to turn my head toward the egress. I observed the orange cat in the doorway through which we had entered the tunnel.

I heard the pounding of drums, *boom-boom-boom-boom, boom-boom-boom-boom*. War drums, hands patting tightly stretched leather. The floor began to vibrate, and the walls made sounds as of seeds in dried gourds—*shhh, shhh, shhh*. Dust descended from the ceiling, and I spat it from my mouth. I tried to balance my weight on my feet as the floor moved beneath them. I shrieked a wordless cry.

"She's here!" I heard crackling over a walkie-talkie, as four or five flashlight-bearing people came through the doorway into my rocky confinement.

They asked if I were okay, and I told them of the sorrowful sounds, and the shaking walls and floors, and the orange cat who had led me to this place.

"I wonder where the cat came from," the leader of the search party wondered. "I've never seen a cat here."

"We need to let maintenance know about the shaking," said another. "We didn't feel anything upstairs."

"I wonder if it is the same pit which the antiquarian recently told us was the place where the Indian maiden was sacrificed a hundred years ago."

"Oh, I know what you're talking about. He said her tribe thought she brought them bad luck, and they tossed her into a pit in the mountainside. That was before the hotel was here."

I asked to be taken to my room, where I packed as swiftly as I could, and I asked the concierge to get me a taxi to drive me into the city, with all due haste.

I have never experienced the desire to see a mountain again.

The Grey House

The grey house is disappearing. The wood is devouring it. I used to see it when I drove by it, but it can no longer be seen that way. I can see it, if I think about it in advance, when I am riding my bicycle past it. I must consciously slow down, and then look for it as I pedal by.

The trees have grown up around it, and in front of it, all the way to the road. To all intents and purposes, what was once a front yard is now a small wood. The long, reaching branch of one tree has actually pushed the mailbox to the ground. Other branches grope the chimney with their gnarly twig digits and claw the shingles from the roof, leaving unhealing scratches that fester with moss. A fallen limb has taken out the top half of the chimney, scattering red bricks across the roof and on the lawn like so many blood splatters.

The windows are many-paned, long and narrow. Some are covered with plastic sheeting, portions of which flap in the breeze. They are clouded with grime, and no light from inside or outside the house passes through them.

The muddy drive from the bent-over mailbox to the house is damp, no doubt because the sun can scarcely get a ray in through the wet and rotting leaves suspended from the twining branches. It goes from the small aperture where the unwilling trees part a bit at the road, and it slinks back into the shade at the rear of the house, where a coven of automobiles sit damply in the sodden ground. From where I am looking, they do not appear to be junkers: I see neither rust nor flat tires. Mind you, I cannot gaze too long. It does not seem wise to stop and stare. If they are not abandoned cars, then someone must be living here, or at least coming here sometimes. Whoever it is, I don't want him to see me looking.

Once there was a grey cat sitting at the end of the drive. A mouse was drooping from the sides of its mouth. I imagine mouse whiskers mingling with cat whiskers. Can the cat feel the pounding of the mouse's heart in its mouth? Instead of slowing down, I pedal faster by the house. I wonder if I should choose a different route for my ride. I look over my shoulder. The cat is still there.

I am, however, drawn to this route. Cheerful houses painted sunny yellow, white picket fences, and a garden full of scare-crows in a front yard. In the midst of these, a damp, dark wood of emaciated trees and moldering leaves clinging for life to the sticks that protrude from the rough-barked trunks, sometimes losing their tenuous grips and belly-flopping to the wet dirt. I pedal past the bent-over mailbox and feel warmer, as if the sun shines more brightly on the road before and after the house than in front of it. I see the grey cat, with a robin in its mouth, sitting under one of the sodden trees.

I cannot sleep one night, for thinking about the grey house. I lie on my side in my bed, looking out the window, through which the full moon is brightly shining—so luminous is it that it is almost an albino sun. I rise and dress and go out into the moonlight. I get on my bicycle.

The world is deserted now. Not a window is lit. There are no cars on the road. There is no sound. By the extraordinary incandescence of the harvest moon I am able to see the road, the ruts and the obstacles, almost as in daylight, but now everything is whitewashed by moonlight.

I head past the shuttered stores, the darkened service station, and turn right at the stop sign. My customary route is made mysterious by the night. I get off my bicycle and look around. The scarecrow garden, so exuberant by day, seems sinister now. Impaled straw men, silently screaming.

The grey house lurks down the road, at the next driveway. Quietening my quickening breaths, I walk my bicycle. Clamminess drapes me like a shawl. Within the confines of my chest my heart thuds dully. The shadows within the small forest are at night as opaque as oil. The dirt drive is untouched by light and therefore invisible. The windows of the grey house reflect the moonshine, as if house and moon are engaged in a communion of sorts.

I am seen. Two green eyes flicker from the inky grove.

The door of the grey habilitation opens, and the bleached glow of moonlight fills the portal, projecting from within the house.

A grey-haired woman in a cobwebbed gown looks up at the moon. As I watch her, enthralled, she turns her green oval eyes to look at me.

She turns inside the house, and the door closes after her. The lights in the windows fade. The trees advance.

All I can see now is jet, complete and utter darkness. The absence of light. The house is blanketed with the gloom.

I sense two green eyes watching as I find my bicycle and return home, oppressed by grief.

Beach Shanty

The old house on the beach,
Where gales scrape the paint from the wood before it is dried,
Its skeletal boards bleach,
And its warped shingles fling out at the red, roiling tide,

Crouches under two dunes,
Watching the waves thrashing themselves up into typhoons,
Launching watery harpoons,
Growing strong and upsurging with the pull of two moons,

Watches the scaled sea-beast,
The indigo, twenty-legged, seven-headed mer-beast,
Swim from dark realms due East,
Devour schooners and sailors in grisly blood feast,

Spit out their gnawed-on bones,
Swim south, stirring black whirlpools that suck down the freighters.
Dark night echoes their moans,
As carnivorous eels race grotesque alligators.

Inspired by Nature

Brenda had always loved woods—and the deeper and darker and more remote the wood the better. So when the recent economic downturn had enabled her to purchase a wooded parcel at a reduced price—why, she became the lady of her own dark manor, deep in the thick old-growth forest of the Black Mountain in northern New Hampshire. Twenty miles from any town, the streams on her property flowed or trickled down from the mountain, according to the amount of rainfall. The countless tall trees' branches intertwining thickly high above her head wove a branch-and-vine lattice that permitted small glimpses only of blue sky in day, or moonlight at night. There was no clearing until she reached the end of her long, winding dirt driveway. In her wood Brenda erected a rustic log cabin and furnished it simply and comfortably. She passed many pleasing weekends and holidays in her wood, dividing her solitary hours between reading and rambling under the trees.

She judged her sanctuary a suitably creepy lair wherein to write the ghost stories that had made her a popular author. Endowed by nature with a gift for storytelling, and with a macabre sensibility, Brenda thrilled to the gloom of the dark forest. She would often make up stories as she walked in it. A winging owl presaged doom, for instance, as it flew overhead with a mouse in its claws. The violets on the moist forest floor might be poisonous plants awaiting a wandering village girl—mayhap her swain would pluck a nosegay for his sweetheart and they would both die for love. In no time Brenda came to know her wood well. Once she spied a crooked and forked branch that had dried up and fallen from the high limb of a tree—only to become caught upon a lower branch; when she had tried to pull it down, she succeeded only in breaking the end off. Neither did the high winds that oft came with the periodic nor'easters dislodge it. In her head she wove a tale that the forked branch was a pernicious omen of death and destruction.

Thus Brenda, weaver of frightening tales, beguiled her forest holidays in her enchanted grove on Black Mountain. Her pen and her keyboard were seldom idle as they strove to keep pace with her imagination. She placed the end of her pen between her teeth for a moment and thought about the friends whose arrival she was anticipating for a celebration of All Hallows on the night of the morrow.

*

Her friends, her agent Jean and Jean's husband Bill, were driving in from Portland the next day to listen to her read her newest story, "Young Love"—a tale that had grown out of her musings on poisonous violets—and they were bringing a holiday repast with them. Earlier that morning she had carved a trio of Jack-o'-Lanterns to put in the windows and on the small porch, and she had put the wine in the refrigerator to chill. Now she was hard at work, polishing the third draft of her story. She stopped writing to scratch an itchy place on her elbow. A spider bite. *How seasonal,* she thought. *I hope the spiders made a freaky web for my party.* Brenda amended another sentence in her manuscript and then bent to scratch her ankle. Another spider bite. She made a note on her reminder pad of paper to call an exterminator the next day—*atmosphere or no atmosphere.* Absently she brushed her cheek with the back of her hand and knocked a large, spotted black spider from her face onto the paper on the table in front of her. With a shout she jumped from her chair, knocking her work onto the floor. She picked up a book and smashed the arachnid into a red pulp, spoiling the draft of her story (she was thinking what she might do with spider blood in one of her stories, even as she cleaned up the mess with a paper towel). When she tossed the paper into the waste can she saw dozens of baby spiders emerging from the baseboard in the kitchen. Brenda looked into the cupboard for an insecticide, which she began to apply liberally to the baseboards. There wasn't enough left in the aerosol can. When she looked up and around, she saw that the room was filling with infant spiders. She picked up her coat and went out.

Pausing outside her cabin, Brenda recollected that in the storage shed she could probably find what she needed, and she turned her steps that way. It was late in the year, and the sun was setting early; the shadows of the forest were growing long.

As she approached the double-doored tool shed, she was forced to duck—a screeching owl was flying toward her head. By a quick maneuver she was able to avoid it. Already darkness was laying claim to the wood, and Brenda returned to her cabin with the can of insecticide. She looked up at the waning orange-red of the sky, which was filtered through the dense branches.

When she lifted her eyes to appreciate the beauty of the setting sun, Brenda was surprised to spy another forked branch hanging over the limb of another tree. After she had taken a few steps more, she observed a third forked branch suspended on another tree's bough!

She entered the cabin and doused the baseboards, dealing death to the spiders, after which she opened the doors and windows to let in the chill autumn air and let out the poisonous fumes. The night sky was rapidly changing to an inky black hue as she replaced the insecticide can in the outbuilding and secured its double doors. Behind the canopy of the branches a full moon glowed numinously, its beams ensnared by vegetation. As she gazed upon the taciturn moon, Brenda was astonished to behold another forked branch—dangling from the bough—of *another* tree! She looked from tree to tree, and by the fluorescence of the moon she could see that there was a forked branch suspended from a bough—*in each and every one of the trees!* Brenda spun around, and in every direction she could see forked branches poised on the limbs of all the trees.

She ventured a little further down the path on which she had so often walked. Milky moonlight continued to disclose tree after tree bearing forked branches among their limbs. The story weaver was becoming spooked by the fantastic premise of her own story: forked branches placed ominously on the boughs of trees to signify doom.

Brenda rushed to her cabin, locked the door, and immediately tucked herself into bed, burrowing beneath the warm quilt to read. Snug in her pile of pillows and cocooned by warm blankets, she fell into a dreamless sleep.

*

She awoke coughing—suffocating. She gripped the edge of the mattress as the coughing racked her body. Bending over, she strove to clear her lungs. She opened her eyes, but she had to close them again, for they burned so badly. Then she touched her face—it felt hot and swollen to her fingertips. Through the slivers of inflamed eyelids she could see the black smoke. The air was blistering. She could hear the fire—the sounds of wood crackling and falling. Her eyes swelled shut, she felt for the door. Once her hands found the door frame, she willed her burning eyes open.

A shaggy, long-haired black goat was standing before her— standing on its hind legs. Its curled black horns swayed wildly as the goat thrashed its bewhiskered neck. It gnashed its teeth and saliva ran in gobs from its jaws. It was blocking the doorway!

Blindly, Brenda reached for the bureau, trying to steady herself. But, as flames started from the wall, she was forced to withdraw her arm, and she knocked off the bureau a bottle of holy water, a housewarming gift. The blaze diminished, and the snarling beast dissolved into the smoke.

Emerging from the charred and blackened cabin, Brenda stumbled to the ground. She clutched a nearby oak tree to pull herself up, but her legs were disinclined to support her weight. She was dazed and foggy—gaseous, immaterial. The rough bark of the tree scratching her palms gave her some slight comfort— this was something solid—and she too was real, for she could feel the tree's texture and could lean her weight upon it.

On jelly legs she ran to her car and pulled her keys from under the floor mat. Starting the engine, she placed the car in reverse and backed it onto the driveway. She shifted into drive and depressed the accelerator. Suddenly she turned the wheel to the left to avoid the great pine tree that was falling into her path, right across the drive—and her front bumper hit a great oak tree. As her head hit the steering wheel, a shower of acorns fell from above. Scores of cawing crows alighted from the tree and hovered between her and the moon.

*

Brenda came to, pinned beneath her car, her legs trapped. She felt her pockets to find her cell phone—it was not there— she tried to determine the severity of her injuries. She was in pain, of course, but was that the extent of it? Broken bones? Paralysis? Impending death? She tried to take inventory of her body. *At least Bill and Jean will be driving by here tomorrow—I should be found by them, if I'm not able to get out of here on my own.* She tried to derive some comfort from that thought. The pain was a good sign—her legs might be okay again in the end—*pain was better than no feeling at all.* She lay trapped, tearfully trying to summon some reason to hope.

Her eyelids flew open—she raised her head—*Voices!* In the distance, in the dark wood, she could hear human voices! "Help!" she called. "I'm hurt. Please help me!" *She would be rescued!*

*

The increasing volume of the voices indicated that the people were coming closer. As they drew nearer, their indistinct murmuring began to sound more like chanting. Brenda continued to shout for help. She saw a group of a dozen, maybe thirteen, hooded people in long red robes approaching. Each was carrying raised high before him a forked branch. Brenda froze, horrified. Continuing their rhythmic chant—Brenda could distinguish the words "blood" and "mountain"—the cowled group encircled her and the wrecked car that held her fast. The circle of hooded figures parted to reveal a black goat—a black goat walking on its hind legs and waving its curled black horns. It gnashed its teeth, and gobs of saliva were dripping down its shaggy chin.

The House

It was always cold in the penumbra of the great old house. Away from its shadows, the yellow autumn sunlight warmed the skin, cheered the heart, and invigorated the body. Nearer to the house, the spectre of its shade raised goose pimples, so that a person might button up his sweater or zip up his jacket as he approached the ancient edifice; indeed, coming from the sunlit street into the shadowy yard, people had often complained of a chill. They would feel depressed, too—saddened for no imaginable reason—and they would tell themselves that the change in their mood was the result of the gloom of the shade. With its many long, lanky Victorian-window-eyes, whose eye-window-shades were half-drawn, as if the house were half-asleep, the rotund edifice would glower upon visitors, would stare without blinking until a person felt quite out of sorts. But it was when a person neared the red-brick monstrosity, came under the spell of the shadow it cast upon the yard, that his skin would crawl. The house had not been lived in for as long as anyone in the vicinity could remember; thus, visitors were an infrequent event.

Some time past, a meter reader from the water company, new in his position, was having trouble locating the meter. As he circumambulated the old manse in search of the dials, he perforce walked in its shadow, peering behind hedges grown wild and the woodpile of rotten logs. The people of the neighborhood will swear that they heard an ungodly, high-pitched scream moments before they saw the water company employee running from the back yard of the house to his truck, which was parked in front of the house, but across the street from it. Pedestrians and motorists alike testified that the man crossed the street—running directly into traffic—and that his death was a direct result of his failure to look both ways before attempting to cross the street.

Generally, people will walk or jog or push their baby strollers on the sidewalk across the road from the house, and not ever on the sidewalk on the same side of the road as the house. The new family in the neighborhood had not been informed of this peculiar detail as yet, when their six-year-old daughter, Lily, rode her new blue bike with the training wheels not only on the sidewalk on the same side of the street as the red-brick house, but up the very driveway of the house, and around the back of it, disappearing from sight into the black shadow which pervaded the property.

Mary and Douglas, Lily's parents, had been planting tomatoes in the garden of their new home, three blocks from the dreadful old house. They had noticed how it glowered when they drove past it, on their way to the post office or the supermarket; they had exchanged remarks regarding their mutual inclination to steer clear of an old ruin that made them shudder to look at. They had thought that perhaps the expansive, three-story Italianate house sheltered drug dealers or some other type of hoodlums. Mary thought the vines that climbed the walls and wound around the peeling porch rails seemed malicious or poisonous. Both Mary and Douglas conceded, when they happened to remark upon it, that they might be the victims of their own fancies. Except when they drove by it, neither gave the red-brick house much thought.

Lily had been climbing trees in the back yard all day, carrying her Barbies in her pocket, making them tree-dwellers for the purposes of her play. When she became stuck on the way down, she called for her mommy and daddy to help her out of the tree. Once she had safely landed on the ground, she and Barbie commenced the baking of an apple pie, the ingredients of which were mud for the crust and an apple she had picked from the tree and placed in her pocket before she got stuck. When the parents were finished with their gardening for the day, they brought their daughter inside, washed her up, put her to bed, and began to prepare dinner while she napped.

Lily, however, did not nap for very long. The warmth of the orange-yellow sun streaming through her bedroom window called her to play outside. She donned clean shorts and a tank top and went out the back door. Seeing her new blue bicycle leaning against the side of the house, she went for a ride. There was a whole new world to explore, for Lily had never ridden past the next house before, had never crossed the street (although she did know that, whenever she did, she must look both ways first). She was not a timid child, by any means, and she was in the clutches of an exciting new feeling—a desire for adventure.

It was thrilling—the feel of her silky blonde hair being blown by the wind as she rode her robin's-egg-blue bicycle, her doll in the wicker basket that was threaded with pink ribbons and attached to the handlebars, spreading her infantile wings. She had always been well loved, had felt secure, had never known fear nor reason to be nervous before—and so it never occurred to her to think twice about riding up the driveway of the very high, red-brick house with the spiky wrought-iron widow walk on top and so many windows on its three floors, and it never occurred to her that maybe she should abjure the dark shadows in which it was bathed.

Lily wished she had had the forethought to wear a jacket, though, because when she rode into the shadow she became very cold. She thought that maybe she would ride around the house and then go back home, for it was dark behind the house. As she rounded the corner, past the brick porch with the porch rail with peeling white paint, she forgot about the temperature—for she had found the back yard.

Unlike the rest of the land on the estate—whose neglected lawns were tinted black and blue in the heavy gloom that ever hung over them—the grass behind the old house was soft and green, and freshly mowed. And, although all the rest of the grounds on which the house sat were shrouded in ponderous shadows, the cheery autumnal sun was shining directly upon a pink and white candy-striped swing set in the back yard, its seats, suspended from shiny silvery chains, moving back and forth slowly in the breeze. Jumping off of her bicycle, Lily raced toward the swings. With her foot she pushed off the ground and glided through the air; and, as she swung back and forth, she caught sight of a field of daisies—and, beyond them, a shimmering blue pond.

"Wow," she said, as she leapt from the swing. And as she spoke she saw that all the flowers in the yard turned their faces to hear her.

"Little girl," the wind called to her. Lily looked around to see where the voice was coming from.

"Here." She spun.

"No, here." The child turned again.

"Here, too." Lily was bewildered. She glimpsed little brown figures scurrying among the daisies, rustling the leaves—cats? squirrels?

"Down by the water."

"Come down to the water, little girl." Lily's lower lip was trembling, for she was confused. Who was calling her?

"Look down."

"By your feet."

"Here I am." And Lily, feeling quite shy now, looked down at the ground by her feet. There was a little brown man there, about six inches tall. He was wearing a brown hat and a brown coat.

"Oh!" said Lily.

"I'm a brownie," the little man said.

"A brownie?" Lily asked. "Like a cookie?"

"A kind of fairy," the little man replied. "This is where the brownies live." He spread his arms, to indicate the area of Brownie Land.

"Ohhhh." The daisies all turned their faces toward the little girl, fluttering their petals.

A diminutive brown lady, dressed in a pretty brown dress, peeked out from behind the stalk of a flower. "There are goldfish in the pond," she called.

Lily turned to see who had spoken. "Goldfish!" she repeated, wide-eyed.

"Goldfish," said the little brown man at her feet, nodding his head.

Lily raised her eyes from the man to peer beyond the swing set, to look at the pond.

"You can see them shimmering in the water from here—but you have to get much closer to watch them swim," called the little woman.

"Oh, can I?" asked Lily.

"You can," replied the brownie. "Follow me."

The brownie was borne up on the breeze and glided toward the pond.

"Wait," Lily implored.

"Come," answered the brownie.

Kicking up her sneaker-shod heels in the soft, green grass,

Lily trotted behind the brownie. In the golden glow of the sun the blue pool appeared molten and warm, its waves lapping the reeds at the water's edge. She leaned forward, trying to see the goldfish.

"I can't see the fish," she said.

"Lean in, lean in," the female brownie said. Lily leaned in, her hands on the bank of the pond, and her shoulders leaning forward over the water.

"I see the fish! I see them!" she cried joyfully. She lifted her arms to clap her hands and fell forward, into the pond.

The water was not too deep for her to stand up in, so close to the bank; and it was a credit to her young nerve that she did not panic, but stood up in the mud and tried to pull herself out by holding onto the reeds.

As she grasped a fistful of reeds in each of her hands, though, the reeds broke and the little girl fell backward into the water. Splashing, Lily tried to regain her footing, but the still water was becoming turbulent, frothing, moving in a circular current like a whirlpool. She felt herself being raised up on the water—and then a great mouth—a mouth with jagged teeth rose from the depths and swallowed both Lily and all the water in the pond.

When Douglas and Mary had realized that their daughter was missing, they called the police and searched the neighborhood. Their neighbors joined the search effort. They discovered only her bicycle in the back yard of the dismal old house, half-buried in slimy, black grass that had not been cut in years. In the back yard was a rusty swing set and a large mud-hole that once had been a pond. Lily's body was not found in the mud, not in the house (when the police searched it)—in fact, it was never found. The grief-stricken couple moved to a new city.

The stout brick house seemed a trifle more rotund in after days, and the shades seemed to hang lower in the long, lanky windows, as if the house had grown sleepier that autumn and was having difficulty keeping its long, lanky Victorian-window-eyes open. The uncanny perpetual gloom persists, and residents of the town still avoid walking on the same side of the street.

The Moon Is Made of Cat

The moon is really a furball,
A grey-and-white mottled cat,
Guardian of the high heavens,
Curled up into a spiral,
White whiskers taken for moonbeams
From earthly low vantage point.
Tail curled up underneath her,
Sweeps worlds away when it bristles,
And arching her spine grinds up stars
To millions of crystalline shards.

Weird Women

A Successful Woman Writer

Jillian's first attempts at writing were laborious, halting, and anything but beautiful, but she kept at it. When it chanced that sometimes a brilliant phrase or image would blow her mind, she would deem her work rewarding (*I can be a good writer—I just need to work at it—I ought to be, with my education and a lifetime of devouring great literature!*). In moments of greater objectivity, she would realize that those sparkling bon mots were embedded within reams of ineptitude. But she kept at it. Two—then three—then four years later, words and characters and entire worlds contained therein simply flowed from the point of her pen. At times she would look in doubt at the pages she had written and wonder how she had done it: how *had* she invented plots and created people and written such beautiful phrases? In fact, to be brutally honest, she could not begin to fathom how such mature literature had come from her own fingertips. Jillian ascribed it to practice.

Day after day Jillian would sit at her desk, placing the point of her pen to a sheet of paper, and begin to write a tale. *Today I'm going to write a story about a woman who is a successful writer,* she might say to herself. *Of course, there must be some twist to the plot,* and then she would start writing, not stopping until a story had unraveled itself upon the white rectangles, which, when she read it, amazed her. *How did I come up with all this? How long has this story been inside me, and where did it come from, and why hadn't*

I known it was there before I read it on this paper?

Shaking her head to banish these unnerving reflections, she stood up from the desk and looked out the window. It was getting dark: only noon, it appeared that an autumn storm was looming. Jillian opened the closet door and pulled from it a flannel jacket. She picked up her gloves and sunglasses from the table in the foyer and went out the front door. *How fabulous! Great black clouds blowing in from the horizon—how they billow as the wind sends the brown and orange leaves skittering along the ground.* She mounted her bicycle, hoping to get in an hour's ride before the rain was loosed. She bade her mind be free, focusing on the rough force of the wind, which was separating the tendrils of her hair and whipping them into her eyes and mouth, and on the straining muscles of her knees and calves, as they pushed the pedals forward and down against the wind. The wind, in turn, assayed to force her bicycle from the road, but she held it in a straight trajectory: Jillian versus the raw fury of Madame Nature. *Let it blow! I am going to finish my ride.* Jillian pushed the pedals, though she had to stand on them to enlist the muscles of her thighs and the weight of her body against the savage energy of the storm.

The successful woman writer is riding her bicycle, as an impending tempest darkens the sky. Gusts of wind snarl her hair, blowing it into her eyes, as she strives against the wind— Stop it! she told herself. *This is not the time to think about the story I am going to write. Jillian, you are going to enjoy your exercise in this splendid moment on the cusp of a tempest, to relax your mind and for a moment be just Jillian, and not an author.*

The cyclist competes for mastery of the bicycle with the frigid gusts, maintaining her vehicle in an upright stance, even as nature endeavors to blow it from under her. Jillian was getting frustrated. *Why can't I think of anything but this story? I'm trying to live in the present, to enjoy this fearsome weather, and to take a night off. Perhaps I ought to see a movie in town tonight, take a break. I've been working day and night.* Jillian, at the crest of a hard-won hill, paused to study the swelling domes upon domes of blackness, swallowing up the grey sky on the horizon. She turned her bicycle and began the much less arduous descent from the hill. She decided that she would stow away her bicycle, repair her ravaged hair, and then go out for dinner and a movie. *The writer is carried downhill, driven by the raging gusts, back toward her house, holding onto the handlebars for dear life. She can no longer steer the bicycle against the wind, blowing now north, now east; all she can do is hold on.—This is crazy.* Jillian tried to push the reverie from her mind. *I am going to order a glass—no, make that a bottle of Amontillado—when I get to the Casablanca Grille. I wonder what the second feature is at the theater.*

Jillian pulled into her drive and secured the bicycle in the garage. Then she went inside the house to change into a dress and repair her hair and makeup. As she reached for her purse and coat, she thought she had better make notes of the ideas that had come to her while she was bicycling. She set the purse and coat down again and walked over to the desk. She leaned over it, scribbling her thoughts for the new story, and then, tired from her strenuous ride, she sat in the chair to continue writing. She glanced at the clock. It was seven o'clock already, she'd better get going—but wait—there were more ideas to write down. Tired and hungry, she could not stop writing, because she kept thinking of the fancies she had had while riding in the coming storm.

Jillian tried to hurry—she really yearned for an evening of fine dining and a film—but *How can I stop when I have so much to say?* She stood up from the chair and turned toward the sofa where she had laid her coat and purse, and then, with a sigh, she turned back to the desk, resumed her seat, and began writing once more.

Rest and food forgotten by now, Jillian began drafting the story of the successful woman writer who marveled at the stories she wrote. *My gifted protagonist cannot imagine where her stories have come from; in fact, the elegance of the prose and plots somehow frightens her—they seem foreign to her. Over time she finds it harder and harder to stop writing, even to leave the house on errands or for pleasure. She ceases interacting with her friends. She even finds it hard to eat anymore, not wanting to stop writing the stories that are pouring forth from her head. She puts the manuscripts into the mailbox on her porch and receives contracts in their place; the publishers always request more of her work. Eventually the mailbox is the only place she will go to beside her desk, and, when she absolutely has to, the bathroom. They find her one day, with her head upon her desk, her hands blackened and shriveled, black bile caked upon her lips. The only words on the paper beneath her palm: Can nothing save me?*

It was morning by now, and Jillian was still at the desk, sleeping in her chair, in the rumpled dress she had donned for an evening on the town. She rose, ambled listlessly to the kitchen, and turned on the coffee pot; and then she returned to her desk, picked up her pen, and began to make notes of the dream she had had while she dozed in the chair, listening to the black form standing at her side, whispering into her ear.

Felinicity

"I'll have the spinach salad with the cauliflower and tofu tempura and candied walnuts, please."

"Sure thing. Have you noticed? That man's been looking at you through the window."

I turn my head to look out the plate-glass window on my right. There's a man with scruffy grey hair and a big grey beard standing there. He's got a long, loose coat on; his hands are in the pockets. As I turn, he turns, his head facing away from me, and walks away.

I pick up my new acquisition, *Malleus Maleficarum,* which I have just purchased at the small bookstore on the next block of the main thoroughfare in this quaint town, and I open the volume to the page marked with the black ribbon that is attached to the binding. There are weird, occult symbols in gold upon the grosgrain ribbon.

My M.O. is to read when I sit in a restaurant. A confirmed bachelorette (I don't care if you think the term sexist—I like feminine terms, because I like being a feminine person; I don't need to be androgynous to be independent or powerful; I wear red lipstick because I like what I see in the mirror when I put it on— not because I give two bits what you think), I often dine alone.

Sipping my unoaked Chardonnay, I start to read about all the ways one can identify a witch. Witches' marks, devil's teats, familiars, the usual litany. Something in my peripheral radar causes me to turn my head—the man is back. He is standing there, hands in his pockets, looking at me through the window. Two young women, both of them looking at the cell phones in their hands, walk by the window, between the man and myself; when they have passed the window, the man is no longer there.

The waitress returns with my salad. I thank her and turn the page of the book and then place the bowl of the spoon on the corner of it so the page doesn't turn while I eat. I pick up my knife and fork, and then the skin on my neck prickles. I turn to see the man at the window again. I raise my hand to call the waitress. When she comes, I ask her to notify the manager about the man. She helps me close the blinds and then goes to the bar to speak with the manager. I watch him go out the front door.

"I apologize, madam, for the man on the sidewalk. Would you like to move to a different table?" he says when he comes back inside. "The man was gone when I went outside to speak with him." The man is indeed gone now, and I have started to eat, so I thank the manager for his assistance and remain where I am.

It is dark when I leave the restaurant. Night comes early at this time of the year. My car (on the trunk of which a bumper sticker proclaims *My Other Car Is a Broom*) is parked three blocks away on the two-lane street that bisects this small town of red-brick buildings with big window storefronts. There are aluminum tables and chairs in front of the restaurant, but no one is sitting at them, because the weather is cold now. The wind is biting, causing me to hold the lapels of my coat closed over my chest. The leaves make a scratching noise on the concrete as they skittle past me on the sidewalk. I hear something. I turn—the man is walking behind me, a block and a half away. I walk faster, arms tensed, purse and coat buttons clutched in my fists, until I reach my car. I push the button on my key. I try the handle: it is still locked. I push the button again and I hear the mechanism click. I toss the purse into the front seat, get in, and pull the door shut. I lock the doors and put the key into the ignition. The car starts. I pull out of the parking space and glance quickly at the rearview mirror—the man is walking on the sidewalk. I drive away, without looking back again. The fool.

"Pyewacket, darling," I whisper in between the kisses I lavish upon the sweet black face of my sleek black cat, who always comes to the door to greet me when I return home. (Yes, I stole her name from *Bell, Book, and Candle*—my favorite movie. I admire the grace and felinicity of Kim Novak.)

Putting Pyewacket down upon the maroon velvet chaise in the living room, I hang my coat in the hall closet and then go into the bedroom to take off the ice-blue silk sheath dress I am wearing and my underthings and don a green embroidered satin dressing gown. Then I go to the kitchen, where I open a can of tuna for Pyewacket and pour a glass of Moet & Chandon for myself. I curl up on the sofa with my new book, pleased by the white light of the street lamps against the inky blackness of the sky outside the picture window.

A car door slams shut out on the street, and so I rise to look out the window. I see the man who was at the window of the restaurant. He is standing next to the car. Now he is walking toward the house. My first thought is that I am not dressed for a visitor and I should dress hastily. And then I think I should not answer the door to the strange man anyway. I look out the corner of the window, trying not to allow the interloper to see that I am watching him. I do not want any trouble. Why can't he just mind his own business? He does not come to the front door. I see him slither around the corner, toward the back of the house, and then I lose sight of him. Are the patio doors locked? They usually are, but of course, every once in a while I forget to lock them. (Who doesn't sometimes forget to lock a door?) I hear a noise at the French doors of the patio.

I whisper, "Pyewacket," and hurry into the bedroom, Pyewacket at my heels. I sit upon the tufted bench at the Louis XVI vanity and open the embroidered jewel box on the top of it. There is a revolver in the box, loaded but never used. Next to it is a velvet pouch. I quickly remove the pouch from the box and pull the strings. I extract a waxen figure from it, a sallow little man. I sprinkle some catnip over the little man and place him upon the floor. You know what happens next: Pyewacket slathers the little guy with her kitty saliva, rolls around the powder-blue carpet with him in her claws. In pussycat ecstasy, she begins chewing the wax.

I hear screams from the patio; the pitch is awful, a tortuous sound. The glass windows of the French doors crash into the house, spraying pieces of glass upon the mosaic tile floor of the solarium. The screaming continues: high-pitched, loud, and wailing now. I praise Pyewacket: "Good girl. My darling does enjoy her catnip, doesn't she?" Pyewacket bites the arm off the figure and carries it out of the bedroom in her teeth, her head and her tail held high.

The screams grow louder, more animal now than human. I follow Pyewacket to the solarium. She goes up to the man, who is writhing on the tiles, crunching shards and plates of glass as he rolls and screams. His arm lies across the room, cloven from his body by a large piece of glass. There is a river of crimson gore between the man and his arm.

I return to the living room, take a sip of delicious French Champagne from the Cristobel flute, and call 911:

"I want to report a break-in. A burglar came in my house through the French doors. He injured himself when he broke the glass."

I carry my Champagne to the solarium, careful not to step in the glass in my satin slippers and cut my feet. I settle into a wrought-iron chair with blue and white cushions and pat my lap. Pyewacket leaps into her place, and we watch the man as he bleeds to death. I wonder if I will be able to clean the tile, or if it will have to be replaced. As the sirens approach, I return to the kitchen to refill my glass.

The Beldame

The silk-shod foot slips in the clay.
Surprised, I leap out of its way.
The lass, careening through the glen,
Has wandered from the realm of men.
I draw in air and puff my face
And bellow out a belch in bass.
My fellow toads heed my alarm

And carry it from swamp to farm,
Croaking a swelling tympany,
"Harrumph Brrrackk"—foul symphony
With which soprano plaints do merge:
"Alas, alack! What evil scourge
Doth beset a maiden's virtue?"
The raven's caw, opossum's mew
The beldame of the Black Wood hears,
Having lived sixteen thousand years.
I leap from twig to branch to leaf,
Hurrying to watch the mischief
That awaits a foolish maiden
Who hath strayed into the black glen
Where dwells the awful sorceress.
Sprawled lies the damsel on the moss,
Tripped up by gnarled roots which cross
The forest floor, her ankle broken.
"Ambrosia, sweet," her name spoken
She looks around and sees four score
(Or more) red pairs of eyes before
Her and behind her in the gloom
And listens to our dour croaking,
Fearing what the night is cloaking.
A bent, old crone repeats, "Ambrosia,"
Slithering closer to the girl
Whispering, "I've caught a squirrel,
A tasty morsel I shall roast.
Of all of you I like the most
Your dainty fingers that I'll wear
Around my neck, strung with your hair."
The wood enlivens with the song
Of mouse and frog and buzzard throng.

The crescent moon smiles crookedly,
Glows on the damsel luridly.
The Black Wood is a festal place
For those of an unearthly race.

Lady of the Lake

Erin went to the lake, summoned by the primeval mists that rise
at night from the cool water and waft from the untrodden grass
and from the moist, black clay of the bank that rings the opaque
pool. After sunset, a swirling fog-cloud swaths the body of water
in the ancient wood within its vaporous veil, concealing the lake,
so that once in a while upon a moonless night, an unsuspecting
late-night or early-morning walker tramps right into the water
and returns home damper than he set out. Erin liked the cool
damp of the mist upon her skin, the damp that wet her shoes
and made her arms cold so that she shivered a little; and she
liked the loneliness, the dearth of human society, which so rude-
ly positions itself between a person and the natural world—the
real world—of which she felt herself to be a part, and from
which most people are always endeavoring to separate themselves. When it was too late and too dark to ply her needle, by
which she earned her living as a seamstress, and when she was
less likely to be observed, Erin walked to the hidden lake. And
when the moon gave but small light and the stars did not twin-
kle as they might, Erin followed the fireflies as they winged toward the water.

At the close of a day of orders and fittings, her close chamber
reverberating with chatty gossip and complaints, it was the chir-
ruping of the crickets and the rumbles of belching frogs for
which she longed, and the choir of warbling and trilling unseen
night birds. When their hymn was sung softly, *piano*, she could
hear the breeze caressing the lake and the lake rippling in reply.

Then she would remove her shoes and stockings and walk in the grass, gratified by the squeeze of the wet earth between her toes. Sometimes, when the moon made the world burn ashen-white, she fancied that she could see nymphs frolicking among the lily pads. Some nights she fell asleep amid the reeds on the shore, wrapped warmly in her woolen cloak, and the sun needed to wake her in time to repair her dishabille and to open her shop. As the years went by, Erin found it increasingly difficult to return to her home and the other world.

*

"My dear girl, you simply must have it ready by tomorrow morning," insisted Mrs. Clarke. "I mean to wear it to Lady Rochester's bazaar for the benefit of poor young ladies in need of modest clothing. It is necessary that the fringed and beaded reticule be ready on time, too, for it matches the new dress in the most darling fashion."

Murmuring her assent, Erin was endeavoring to shepherd Mrs. Clarke to the door, planning to turn the lock in it and to pull the widow shade down on it, just as soon as the woman had walked through it and into the unpaved lane. As she opened the door to let her customer out, though, a singularly appealing gentleman materialized in the doorframe. The gentleman bowed to Mrs. Clarke, addressing her as "Aunt," and then reached out his hand to take her purchases from the seamstress and stuttered, "Th-thank you, miss," unable to withdraw his gaze from her countenance.

"Your eyes," he faltered. "I . . ."

"Sir, are you all right?" Erin asked.

"What is your name?" the gentleman asked.

"Erin, sir."

"I beg your pardon. Please allow me to introduce myself. I

am Michael Clarke, Mrs. Clarke's nephew."

"Speaking of which," his aunt replied, clearly irritated, "if you don't clear the doorway, Michael, neither of us shall make it home before dinner is either burnt or cold."

"Pardon, Aunt. Let us hasten to our delicious repast. Good evening, miss."

Bidding them good night, Erin fastened the door; and within minutes she had wrapped herself in her cloak, tucked a loaf of bread and an apple into its deep pockets, and absconded to the wood, impatient to put distance between herself and the world and desirous to return to the hidden lake.

Delighted to find that the night was warm for April, Erin hung her cloak upon the limb of a twisted tree and skipped into the veil. Every night the mist rose from the land and from the water; every night the lake vanished; and nearly every night Erin entered the mist to be with the lake. Long ago she had wondered at her actions, so different from the habits of the people she knew, but she had stopped questioning her need for the pool in the wood: she felt whole when she was with it and, when she gave it a thought, she wondered at the rest of the world. Was there any purpose to it?

An owl hooted in the gloom, and squirrels stirred the leaves in their scrambles, while Erin sat upon a log and ate her bread and fruit under the stars, relishing her humble fare. When she was finished, she emptied the crumbs from her apron into the black lake to feed the fish, which she never could see in the dark. Of the other water creatures she did, however, sometimes catch fleeting glimpses, and, on rare nights, she even heard their whispers. Fairies or naiads, she knew not what they were, but it pleased her to watch and to hear them: they belonged to the lake she loved. She made her bed among the broad and tangled roots of an ancient yew.

When he rose from his own bed, golden Apollo waked her softly; and, not long after, as Erin was opening the door of her cottage to finish Mrs. Clarke's gown, she was startled by a masculine voice at her elbow.

"Good morn, Miss Erin. Pray forgive me for intruding so early in the day."

It was the dapper gentleman, Mrs. Clarke's nephew.

"Good day, sir. How may I help you?"

Instead of answering, the young man stared.

"Twin pools," he uttered at last. "Two lakes, rippling in the breeze. Your eyes, I mean. No—*I am not mad!* I am merely and utterly taken with your eyes. I've no doubt that many have told you of their beauty."

"No, sir. None before now. Pardon me, but I must get to work."

Michael had never been so besotted. Blond and sapphire-eyed, with a noble profile, an upright bearing, and a pleasing manner, it was no wonder that he quickly became Erin's suitor. Initially she was distracted by his wooing—by his praises and his learned conversation, by his willingness to flout the strictures of class, by his honest nature, and by his kisses. He at first had only been bewitched by Erin's black eyes, in which he fancied he saw the pools of dreams—now still and promising, now rippling and alive—but he soon came to know Erin's goodness and understanding. He would not have given her up for the world. Michael could twist his aunt, who doted on him, around his little finger, and so, eventually, he asked Erin to be his wife.

Alarmed, Erin resolved to flee. To be a wife would mean to give up her lake! She would no longer sleep under the moon, no longer recline among the roots of the twisted trees on the shore. Nor would she spy nymphs among the fishes and listen to owl-and-cricket choruses. She would never again leave the world of people. Ever.

At evenfall Erin slipped quietly from her cottage. This time, though, she left a note for Michael, stating that she deeply regretted having to decline the offer of his name and his hand, that it was impossible for her to offer an explanation, and that she did not know when she would return. That night, carrying extra food with her, she absconded into the mist.

Michael arrived in time to witness Erin's flight—and he followed her into the wild wood.

With a flurry of feathers, a flock of shrilly squawking black birds burst skyward from the trees, and the discord of the leaves that rustled in their wake mingled with the fluttering of their wings, generating an almighty commotion in the black wood. There was no moon that night. Wary owls telegraphed their neighbors that a man had entered the wood. The man, made circumspect by the profusion of night sounds, picked his steps with care in the dark, continuing in the direction Erin had taken. Briars plucked at his sleeves and roots tried to trip him, but Michael persevered, holding onto branches when his boots slipped in the wet clay. He knew the mist, rather than saw it, for his hair grew damp and droplets beaded on his face.

A beautiful note caused him to halt—a sigh, a note, a song. He resumed his search for the songstress, cautiously lifting his foot high with each step to avoid getting caught in the undergrowth and testing the ground before he put his weight down, because there was no light; and yet, despite all his care, he ran straight into a massive stone. Instinctively touching one hand to his smarting nose, he rummaged with the other in his pocket and withdrew his matchbox. By the dwarfish flame of the match he discovered a face graven upon a strange, rectangular monolith which had been hewn from a mystical mountain.

Two lines for eyes, two sides of a triangle for a nose, a circle for a mouth. *A face from the dawn of time, from before the writing down of history.*

About the monolith he sighted many smaller stones, which were heaped up in a ring—a wreath of rocks around the monolithic face.

The match burnt down and stung his fingers, and he dropped it.

The lovely note sounded again.

As Michael followed the song, the clouds moved away from the moon and the wood became a radiant, white, living thing.

Michael slogged through the vegetation until at last he came to the lake.

He studied the glistening pool, captivated by the slender white limbs emerging from the black ripples. A splash caused him to turn his head. He saw Erin, on the far side of the pool.

"My love, I will come to you. Wait for me," her lover called gently.

When he had walked around the lake to the other side, he took Erin's hand into his own, and his soul went out from him, into the black pools that were her eyes.

"I know why you would not wed me. I love you. Do you love me?"

Erin looked her love with her eyes, and Michael gathered her into his arms.

The mist embraced the lovers.

They never after that came out from the wood.

Madeline

I remember when I first met Madeline. She was sitting at a table, sipping white wine and studying the Egyptian *Book of the Dead*. Her table was across the room from mine, a sea of white linen-covered tables between us. Two of the walls in the restaurant were made of plate glass, permitting a pretty view of the gardens of the Art Museum. A certain species of person tends to make a second home of institutions like museums. I, too, was dining alone.

Although the food is four-star, I had just some bruschetta and two glasses of wine. I was reading a book about Hieronymus Bosch, whose Renaissance paintings of the strange creatures of hell were the most important thing I took away from my undergraduate art history class. When I had drained the second glass, I paid my check and wandered through the Medieval Armor Gallery, and then went on to the Egyptian rooms.

I have always been drawn to the canopic jars, the jars with heads for lids, in which the vital organs were placed when they had been removed from a corpse prior to its mummification. The human-headed jar (representing Imsety, who was associated with Isis) would contain the liver. The jackal-headed jar (representing Duamutef, who was associated with the goddess of war) was the repository of the stomach. The lungs went into a jar with a baboon head (Hapy). Qebehsenuef is the jackal-headed figure on the jar that held the deceased person's intestines.

I turned the corner, so intent upon the canopic jars and the mummified cat next to them that I almost pressed my nose on the glass case, and bumped into Madeline.

"I'm so sorry—I wasn't looking where I was going. I sincerely apologize."

She said that was okay, no harm done. She smiled cordially.

"I saw you in the restaurant," I said. "My name is James Collins, and I'm a member of the museum. I come here a lot."

"It's a pleasure to meet you, James." Her big brown eyes met mine and held them. "I am Madeline Usher."

"I guess we both appreciate the Egyptian collection," I said. "But I don't want to be a pest, so I won't keep you from your browsing. Enjoy your afternoon."

"You aren't a pest, James. If you like, we can study the artifacts together. I'm interested to learn your thoughts."

"I'm no expert, Madeline," I answered, "but I am certainly intrigued by the Egyptian obsession with life after death. It's like they spent all their time living thinking about their next life instead of this one." We moved to a mummy case.

"The pharaohs did not have to think about death and rebirth: they appointed priests and tomb-builders to handle the preparations for them."

"That's true, Madeline. They could consider their futures under control—and enjoy their present lives. That's an interesting insight."

"This mummy looks like an intact body wrapped in gauze, doesn't it?" she asked, as we looked at a woman who had been removed from her coffin. "It's hard to imagine that it is hollow, that her vital organs have been taken from her and replaced with cloth."

We examined the symbols on the coffin, pointing out to each other Osiris, the falcon-headed god, the pharaoh, the priests, the serving women veiled in transparent cloth or in nothing at all. The security guard approached: he politely warned us that the museum would be closing in fifteen minutes. I said good night and told Madeline how much I had enjoyed our discussion:

"Perhaps we'll run into each other here again sometime."

"James, if you like, we could have lunch here tomorrow and resume our discussion," she said, smiling with her lips, her large brown eyes gazing into mine with a singular intensity. I accepted her invitation. We said good night and joined the stragglers who were hastening to the exit lest they be locked in all night.

I arrived an hour early the next day, an hour that I spent sitting in my car in the parking deck, thinking about the fascinating

Egyptophile with whom I would be lunching. I kept recalling her caramel eyes. So very striking, her eyes. At ten minutes of twelve I headed inside the museum.

She was waiting in the lobby. She was wearing a white suit and blouse. On one lapel was a large gold brooch in the form of a cobra, coiled up with its head erect and emeralds for its eyes. In the sunlight-flooded room I noticed the unusual slant of her eyes, which were beautifully delineated with black eye liner. She really is into Egypt, I thought. Maybe she is Egyptian.

We shook hands and walked toward the restaurant. The maître d' showed us to a table near the window.

Over a fine meal and a bottle of wine, we discussed the history of Egypt. I told her that people always seem surprised to learn that Egyptian rulers would often deface memorials to their predecessors; I do not find the practice so remarkable, myself, considering that people have always done so, and that the practice of rewriting history still occurs today. Madeline talked about the *Book of the Dead,* explaining how the First Kingdom Funerary Texts (which had been mainly written on the walls of tombs) had evolved into Coffin Texts (written on coffin lids and shrouds in the time of the Middle Kingdom) and then had become the *Book of the Dead* in the Second Intermediate Period. These tomb texts are magical grimoires that contain spells to ensure a successful transition to the Afterlife; they are found in the tombs of ancient Egypt. As Madeline spoke, I was probably making a fool of myself, for I could not stop staring into her golden-brown eyes. Her velvety voice made me want to listen to her forever. After lunch, we adjourned to the Egyptian gallery.

Madeline showed me some scarabs, inscribed with hieroglyphics. I was astounded, for she was able to translate the inscriptions—spells to enable the deceased to know his own name and retain his identity on the Other Side. She took my hand into hers, holding it as she explained, with zeal, that words possess magic, and that words can bring thoughts into being. I must have scoffed a bit, for she turned her gaze from the artifacts into my eyes:

"Oh, yes, James, words create life, and they bring death, as well," she said, inhaling deeply, as if she needed more air to continue this conversation. "The Egyptians texts hold the key to eternal life—to becoming a god!"

I did not know how to reply, but I desired her to keep holding my hand, so I just nodded. She led me to a bench before a mummy case:

"See that little figure of a man? It is an *ushebti*, a laborer. When we enter the Field of Reeds, we shall require men to work for us there."

"You sound as if you plan to go there yourself, Madeline," I said, speaking to her mesmerizing eyes more than to Madeline herself, for I felt myself falling into their depths. She was still holding my hand. I did not want her to let go—I was even afraid she would let it go. "I think that I would like to go with you—someday, that is—if you go there."

"Oh, yes, James. The warmth and brilliance of the sun there surpasses the most perfect days here. Cool, clear water flows in great rivers over moist and fertile earth, bringing forth the most succulent fruits. Marble palaces and alabaster temples line avenues paved with gold and precious gems. Men and women are gods—beautiful, strong, and powerful! It is something to look forward to, indeed." I expended much effort to heed her words, for, although I loved the tones of her voice, I was painfully aware of the touch of her hand on mine and of the force of her chocolate eyes.

Somehow I found myself alone in the courtyard with Madeline, sitting upon a stone bench. I felt unsure, a little confused. I attempted to make conversation.

"So do you live around here? Are you from this area?"

"I have recently moved here from an old town in New England. I lived with my brother there, in our family home. But my brother has died" (she looked forlorn and touched her hand to her eyes) "and—and our ancestral manor has fallen into disrepair and has been condemned. I long to be reunited with Roderick in another life."

"Dear Madeline, perhaps that explains your preoccupation with the Afterlife." Seeing that she began to shiver, as if distraught, I took her in my arms to comfort her. I started!—She was so cold—ice cold! I drew back.

"Oh, please don't let go. Please hold me. I need your comfort," she implored. I drew her to me once more, and she placed her face on my breast. Moments later she raised her face to mine, saying,

"James, allow me to see your palm please." I was surprised, but I complied with her request.

"I'd like to write on it, if you wouldn't mind. It is a strange request, I know, but it would bring me comfort." I felt a little peculiar, but her eyes had locked mine in a passionate embrace. I could not resist.

"Just a prick—"

I jumped up from the bench and looked at my hand—she had sliced my wrist with her nail and drawn blood!

"What the hell?"

"Darling, just a little more patience, please. You will make us both so happy." My mouth agape, I found myself unable to speak in the presence of those magnificent eyes. She patted the place I had just vacated on the bench. I returned to my seat.

She dipped the long, red nail of her forefinger into the blood, which was running from my wrist. She raised her finger to her succulent lips and licked the blood from her finger. I was beginning to experience some doubts about Madeline.

She dipped her finger into my bleeding wrist once more, and then touched it to my palm. She drew strange figures— hieroglyphs!

"Madeline, what are you doing?" I almost shouted. I pulled my hand, but she would not let it go. She flashed the radiance of her eyes into mine.

"Words are magic. They bring life. I am writing of your rea-wakening as my steward, in the Field of Reeds. I shall have need of your strength when I return there. You will feel no pain, James."

I stared at the falcon head, which she was inscribing with my blood upon my palm—and I realized that a rebirth required a death first. I took back my hand—and I struck Madeline, when she flew at me in an attempt to regain it. She stumbled back, two or three steps, and then drew herself up to her full height in a regal stance.

"Words give life—and death, too, you said! What are you trying to do?"

"James, yield to me. Allow yourself to be drawn to me."

I'd had enough, though. I pulled some tissues from my pocket and bound my wrist. I went straight to my car, never once looking back. I have never returned to the museum, having lost my taste for Egypt. Sometimes I see those crystalline brown eyes, though. Sometimes I cannot not see them.

The Witch

I wear the darkness,
Invisible to unknowing eyes.
I dwell within the deep abyss,
Abide with shadowy stygian skies.

Ravens' feathers my chief adornment,
Crows' wings my dainty fan,
An adder's skin against my flesh,
A pool of oil my looking glass.

I walk in horror—look not away—
Gaze deep, into my rotted heart,
Submerge your will in mine—you are my prey.
I tear your damned soul apart.

Shrieks and howls and screams my song,
Gore and sweat and blood my scent,
Torn flesh and empty skin for which I long—
I feast upon your dying breath.

My robe is spangled with the stars,
Shining, glimmering black jet and pearls.
A field of ice-smooth glass encloses
My deadly beauty, smiling, beguiling.

Round and soft, pliant, inviting you,
I peer around a corner.
You catch a glimpse of mine delights,
Yield yours to mine, forever lost.

I croon, or keen, or crow, or whimper, for
I have snared another man.
A black witch temptress stalking game 'neath
Plutonian skies, in no-man's land.

Diana, Hekate, Lilith, Demeter,
Dark seduction, forbidden prize.
The joy of evil, the lure of misery,
I beckon and lust reels you in.

Monsters in
Our Neighborhood

Leave My Cat Alone!

Each night the howling grew louder. A hideous chorus of elongated ululations. When she returned home from work at midnight and opened her car door, she would hear them. Baying at the moon. Not dogs. Often a pitiful high-pitched yelping emerged in the midst of the chorale, becoming a squeal of great urgency. And then abruptly ceasing.

Each night the sounds came closer to her home. Howling like devils. And then yelp-yelp-yelping that suddenly terminated.

One night she found a fluffy white cat, wet with dew and blood, on her lawn. Its hind legs were broken into weird angles, and its belly was gutted. Forelegs and head remained intact, testimony that it had been conscious when it was eaten alive. She heard the howling, and she picked up the remains of the cat with her snow shovel and placed them in her rose garden. She went inside and listened to the howling until she fell asleep.

She was not able to make it to work in the morning. Fourteen inches of snow had fallen while she slept, and her car was in too deep for her to excavate it. The phone lines were down, and she could not call a snow plow. She was glad that she still had electricity and heat, but she felt the isolation of her log cabin on her twenty-acre spread.

She tried to make the best of an unexpected day off, stoking the wood burner and picking up a book she had been wanting to read. She spent quality time with her aged black cat, Simone. She read and dozed the day away, catching up on much-needed rest. As darkness fell, the howling made her more alert. Simone hunched against her feet, but she would not let the woman pick her up.

"It's okay, Simone, sweetheart. They can't get us. They're outside. We're safe in here, baby," the woman said, stroking the frightened cat.

The tinkling, cracking, crashing brought her to her feet, even before she felt the flying glass. A great grey wolf stood a dozen feet from her on the oval rag rug in her living room, shards of glass all over its coat. The wolf bayed and snarled and snuffed, and drool poured from between its great jaws. It bared its teeth and sprang.

She thought of Simone. Simone was not going to end up like that poor white cat. The woman seized the silver loving cup from the mantel and swung it with both arms and brought it down upon the snout of the beast, who was already in mid-leap. "Leave my cat alone!" she screamed.

The wolf fell to the floor and lay on its side. The woman edged cautiously past the wounded beast to the kitchen, to get her revolver from the utensil drawer, not turning her back to the intruder.

She returned, hugging the wall for support, and switched off the safety on her gun. The giant wolf appeared to be dead already. Holding her gun before her, her arms locked in position and her finger on the trigger, she looked at the wolf to see if it was breathing. She did not detect any rise and fall of its chest.

Then its hair began to recede, its snout grew smaller while its hind legs grew longer, its flesh turned pink, and it became a nude young man. A seemingly dead young man.

The woman did not have any silver bullets, but now that the

werewolf had resumed its human shape, she thought that she could probably finish him off with regular ammunition. She shot him once in the head.

"That's for the white cat," she said.

She shot him in the heart: "And that's for what you tried to do to Simone."

Botched Job

Boris fell to his knees. The wet ground was cold and his knees sank in to it. Having caught his breath, he found it a bit of a challenge to extricate himself from the muck, but with only a little struggle he was back on his feet. Forging deeper into the woods, he pushed back the reaching branches and avoided the grasping roots, thinking that the mud bath was a serendipitous happenstance, for it would cloak his aroma from the empirical noses of the canine contingent.

He had not heard a sound—save his own huffing and the thumping of his heart—for what seemed a very long time. He was probably in the clear. For now. He had time to think what he was going to do next. Boris felt in his pocket, removed the ring—a nice big diamond, set in platinum, a lot of little diamonds on the band. A small fortune. He just had to get it to his customer, who had paid well for the trinket. Very well—for he had known that it never left the lady's finger. Now it had—left the lady's finger.

Of course she had struggled. But he knew what he was about. He had learned her habits, found out when she was usually to be found alone. On Thursday evenings, when her husband was out at his weekly poker game, she usually curled up with her grey tabby cat in front of the fireplace, reading contentedly. He had often watched her, through the sheer curtains on her bay windows, petting the cat on her lap, balancing the book on the arm of the big chair, that rock catching the lights of the fire and the Waterford crystal reading lamp on the table next to her. She wasn't going to get away with that, oh, no, not her, sitting there so smug as if the world owed her a living—and a big rock. He wanted to strangle that cat, that petted cat, sitting there in the lap of luxury. Who did they think they were?

When he felt sure of his plan, he went in through the back door. He had cut the alarm wire, and the lock itself was kid's play. He came up behind her and gave her a good one on the head— slammed her with an onyx statue that he had previously observed standing upon the table in the foyer, which he had decided to use for his weapon. Even as the blood spurted everywhere—like an insane garden hose—she had tried to stand, had raised her arms to shield her head. He struck her again—the cat leapt at his face. Boris tried, but could not snag the animal, and it raced out of the room. He removed the ring from her blood-slippery hand, went into the kitchen, and washed his face and hands, the ring, too. He wiped his fingerprints from the sink and slid the bauble—the classy bauble—into his pocket. As he approached the back door, he heard sirens. Something had gone wrong! He had been so careful, too, thought he'd covered all his bases. He bolted.

Running through the back yards of the row of McMansions, he headed for the street, several blocks away, where he had parked his car. When he emerged from the shrubbery and apiaries behind one executive home with a three-car garage, at the end of a cul-de-sac where he had left his car, he found that the police were already there, two squad cars parked beside his own junker. He avoided the reds and blues flashing on the lawn and ran into the woods behind the houses. He did not think that he had been seen; but the dogs knew he was there and set about yowling and barking—all the dogs in the neighborhood climbing the chain-link fences of their kennels, trying to get at him. Luck was with him, as it usually was, this time in the form of a mud slick.

He walked for fifteen minutes, thinking that soon he would be coming out on the other side of the narrow strip of trees (which go by the name of "wooded lots" in suburbs), but he could not see the edge of the grove. He decided to walk a little more before he stopped, watching for the appearance of halogen-lit asphalt streets or manicured lawns through the leafy branches. Fifteen minutes later he still could not see the other side of the wood. He thought that he must be going in circles. He arranged a couple of branches in strategic places, so that he would know that he was going in circles if he passed by them again. Ten, twenty minutes later—he was still walking in woods, with no sign of the neighborhood surrounding the small park.

He glanced at his watch: it was midnight now. He was supposed to deliver the goods at two o'clock. There'd be hell to pay if he did not make it—he'd already received half down. And the customer was not exactly an understanding sort of guy. He saw a faint glow, a feeble light of some kind—a house! It must be. He began walking quickly in the direction of the beacon. Right into a pricker bush that snagged his pantleg.

Boris fell, landing flat on his face. Initially he was stunned, but he pulled himself together and sat up. He pulled a dirty wad of tissues from his coat pocket and applied them gingerly to his nose. It was streaming with clotting blood and it hurt to touch it—broken! He had not the luxury of time to coddle himself. After he had delivered the goods he could see to his nose. He turned abruptly—he had to get to the light, to get out of the wood.

"Dammit!" A big branch slapped him across the face, sending fire up his broken nose and leaving a great welt across his cheeks. "Careful, bud," he murmured to himself. "You off yourself, you save the man the trouble." He watched his step more carefully, stretching his arms before him to ward off the wicked limbs. "Damn trees. Damn wood," he muttered.

"Hell!" he shouted as he fell again. A furry animal—a fox? a cat? that damned cat!—had dashed between his feet. At least this time he landed on his rump—no harm done. He had to get moving, though, time was running out.

He placed his palms on the sodden, moss-covered ground to push himself up and felt metal. He got to his feet, pulled his mag light out of his pocket (patting the rock again to make sure it was safe), and shone the bright light upon the ground. It was a man-hole cover—in the middle of a wood. *Probably planning to develop it,* he thought. *They can't even leave a little bit of goddamn nature alone.* He started to walk around it, in a hurry, time running out.

Flat on his back! That's how he landed this time.

"What the hell?" He tried to rise, but something had hold of his ankle. It hurt—it was holding him very tight. He reached in-to his pocket again—the mag light, *where is it?* He felt it, pulled it out, fumbled with the switch, flicked it in the right position, and there was light. He turned the beam to his ankle—and he screamed!

A leathery brown paw was holding him by the ankle—it was reaching from the manhole. He picked up a branch—whacked it! whacked it again! It unsheathed rough, ugly claws at least three inches long and gashed a row of deep fissures in his calf.

Boris howled in pain—nonverbal, primeval noises, for he no longer possessed the capacity to employ oaths and blasphemies in recognizable human language. Panting, hyperventilating, trembling in terror, he turned his attention to his voluminous pockets again. Where was his gun—*where was it!* There, there, that pocket. He withdrew it, fired once—twice—three times at the leathery appendage.

The manhole cover moved—a little up, and then to the side, and then rattled as it rolled away from the hole in the ground.

Giggles—he heard giggles! And snuffling, snorting, slurping—he heard those, too.

His nostrils flared, his chest expanded fully—rose so high and fell again with each breath so that he could not ignore his own breathing—as if his body were telling him to take care that each breath might not be the last. He experienced the paralysis of dread—the numbing that starts in the groin and spreads through the trunk and limbs, until you are frozen with terror. He aimed his gun into the hole and emptied the magazine. Boom! Boom! Boom!

His ears hurt now as much as his nose and his leg—and his head rang with the reverberations of the shots in the close chamber. He must have got the sucker this time! He relaxed a very little—exhaled—and, using both hands, tried to pull his injured leg from the razor-sharp shackles.

In one great, swift motion, the Beast rose from the subterranean den—a leathery, brown, demonic abomination with wings that spread at least twelve feet and were taller than Boris, who was six foot three. It reared its head, baring two long rows of incisors like barn nails, and yodeled an atrocious cry that was not of this world. Upon six leathery legs, which terminated in the aforementioned talons, it crawled from its loathsome burrow.

Long past the point of speaking, Boris babbled and sobbed, willing himself to breathe, his breaths coming ragged now, quite undependably. His eyes darted to and fro, seeking an escape, a rescuer—a miracle. He held his breath: he could see a pair of eyes in the charcoal void of the wood—*cat's eyes*. The tabby cat was sitting upon a stump, regarding the proceedings with some interest, as the creature began to eat Boris's intestines.

Cosplay

"I'm going to punch your face in, so help me—"

Jack was yanked back by a young man pulling on each elbow. "Let me go!"

"Oh, Jack, lighten up. How could your best friend resist such an opportunity? Shake hands," Roseanne said and blew him a kiss, for she was safely beyond his reach.

"Sorry, Jack. It was a chance I couldn't pass up—you bent over, your face in the water, bobbing for apples. Sorry, Bud. I really am." Mike laughed so much that he started coughing, and he stepped behind Roseanne, placing his hands on her arms to hold her like a shield before him.

Wiping his wet face and dripping hair with a bunch of orange and black paper napkins, Jack said, "Well, you owe me. I guess it would have been hard to resist," and he slapped his friend—hard—on the back.

"I'll buy you a drink—although our beloved Evans City Grange has put together this super Halloween party." Mike's voice dropped to a whisper. "Behind the haystack is where the real party begins. I know where someone has stashed a fifth of vodka and a six-pack of brew, in the haystack at the far end of the parking lot."

"Come on, Jack, buy Mike and your thirsty sister a drink," said Roseanne, as she led the way to the coat rack. "Let's say our goodbyes, go out the front door, and then sneak around back."

*

"You know how to tell when you've had too much?"

"No, Jack, tell us," answered Roseanne.

"When a scarecrow starts to look good to you."

"Valerie will be here from NYU for winter break in six weeks. Think you can keep your hands off the scarecrow till then, bro'?"

"Man, Mike, a guy can dream, can't he?"

"You know what I dream about sometimes? *Seriously,* I mean?" asked Mike.

"What?" Roseanne batted her eyelashes at him. "Me?"

"Crop circles. I'm not kidding. *Crop circles.*"

"Put the bottles in this bag, and then let's go."

"What's the hurry? Where are we going, Jack?" asked Mike.

"To make crop circles, dude. Let's cruise down to Ash Stop Road and do some landscaping in the cornfield there. On the way here I saw a big John Deere sitting all by its lonesome in the field. Let's give the corn a haircut."

"Cool," replied Mike.

"I'll ride shotgun," said Roseanne, stroking Mike's hips through his tight jeans.

"I'll ride shotgun. You ride sidesaddle," replied Mike, and she feinted an uppercut to his chin.

*

"I told you shop class is cool. It teaches you how to hotwire cars—and tractors. Let her rip, baby."

"You're so manly when you steal a tractor, Mike," Roseanne cooed tipsily.

"Remember, there's a chaperone tonight—me, kiddies—so save those games for when you're alone."

"Okay, big brother. Boy, this corn is tall."

"It looks like it's rotting," Jack said, fingering a stalk. "It's red—ooh, and it's slimy. Hey, this corn has got red stuff—looks like it's got blood on it. Look!"

The others came over and inspected the corn he was fingering.

"This one, too," said Roseanne, moving down the even row of stalks. "They're all covered with red slime. I smell something gross. Do you smell it, too?"

"Yes," the two young men answered at the same time.

"I heard a noise—over there," said Jack.

"Shh," said Mike. "Get down."

They hunkered down to the ground.

"Aaagh!" screamed Jack, his blood spraying all over Roseanne and Mike, as a grey-fleshed woman in a tattered and faded housedress bit a chunk off the side of his face.

Mike and Roseanne pulled on his arms to get him away from the carnivorous housewife—but a hairy arm, enclosed in the sleeve of a policeman's uniform, emerged from the line of stalks and gripped Roseanne's shoulder. She screamed—Mike turned to her. He punched the arm to make it release its hold on her. Instead, it tore the left arm from her body! Mike picked up his girlfriend's limp form and ran with it to the car.

Covered in the blood of his two friends, all he could think of was saving himself and Roseanne. He ran as fast as he could, burdened by her slight body, watching her life running out with her blood. Before he reached the car, he stopped short.

Between him and the car were a dozen grey-hued people dressed in tattered and blood-spattered garments. They walked toward him with slow, shuffling steps, their arms outstretched before them. *This can't be real,* he thought: *there's no such thing as zombies.*

He then recollected that this field was the field where they filmed that classic zombie movie that his parents raved about. He looked again at the horde, trying to decide if he should try to rush the line of zombies.

He recognized the guy in the front of the mob. Who was that? Oh, yeah, Bill. Bill was a nerd who liked cosplay, dressing up like Dungeons and Dragons and things. Mike used to laugh at his absurdities. He recognized Shelly—and Peter—he knew these people. *They weren't zombies.* Hell, he needed to get Roseanne to the hospital, and no weirdo kooks were going to stop him.

"Thanks for coming to our private Halloween celebration," Bill said, and the pack continued their slow advance toward him. "Usually we use dress-shop mannequins as our victims when we re-enact the zombie march through the field to the farmhouse. Tonight, though, we get to cosplay with real flesh. What a trip!"

"You're crazy!" screamed Mike, as the teenage horde pushed him down and fed upon him and Roseanne.

Inspiration

Ron was tired, but he was on a roll and dared not stop. His brilliant plot, his sublime imagery, his consummate characterizations—only through hyperbole could he express his amazement at the quality of his own work. He knew that he was putting out some pretty good stuff—praiseworthy plots, some displaying uncanny insights—but interspersed with mediocre to downright amateurish efforts. Sure, he wrote ceaselessly, whenever he had a moment to spare, and the outcome of so much practice was that he had become a good writer. Yet his writing was so much more than that, which explains his bewilderment. He felt that practice alone could not account for the high caliber of his work.

"Ron, are you ready yet?" Sarah called from the living room. "Ron?"

Damn, he had forgotten. He had agreed to take his wife to dinner. His fingers plied the keyboard more swiftly. Frantically.

"Ron," from the hallway now. She had almost reached his office.

"Ron—you're not ready!" She was in the room.

"Oh, Sarah. Hi. I forgot about our plans. Give me five minutes and I'll be ready. First, though, let me jot down some ideas so I don't forget—"

"Ron, Bev and Gerald are meeting us there. I don't want to be late."

He was beginning to get angry.

"Five minutes, Sarah," he said softly, as he headed toward the bedroom.

*

"Ron, relax, bud. You're working too hard," Gerald said. "Put away your notebook and join the party."

Frowning, Ron replaced the small notepad in the inner pocket of his sports coat.

"How have you been, Ger? Have you and Beverly done much traveling since we last met?"

Sarah and Bev exchanged concerned glances. What was going on with Ron? He was so distant, difficult to engage beyond perfunctory small talk. They had all been friends for years, since their college days.

"Your wife tells us that you've enjoyed a well-deserved success with your writing this last year. She tells us you've been working day and night."

"Yes, thank you. I've been satisfied with my work this year, and it has received some good reviews, too."

Ron thought about the pen and paper in his pocket, wishing that he could make notes about the frustration and irritation he was feeling. People were always getting in your way when there were things you wanted to do. He envisioned a red-faced man curling his hands, and he felt the tension coursing through the man's body beneath the covering of his skin. He wanted to describe—no, he wanted to pour out the words, phrases, and images crowding his mind into the computer on his desk at home—an angry man's physical sensations—the icy cold of his hands, the feeling as if one's head and trunk were swelling balloon-like. The man's face would be tense—his mouth a grimace, lips firmly placed together, teeth unclenched behind his lips. His character's eyes, squished beneath a bulging forehead, would gaze into nothingness. The man's nostrils would flare as he sucked air deeply through the twin nares into his lungs. From his shoulders to his hands would flow red heat. As the character he was developing fixated on the object of his fury—became saturated with his own anger—he would *see* the red color of the heat.

"Earth to Ron." Sarah caressed his bristly cheek, bringing him out of his reverie. "I'm afraid you *have* been working too hard. I probably shouldn't have urged you to come out tonight. You would have benefited from a quiet night at home."

Checking his stronger impulses, Ron admitted to fatigue. Said he should probably turn in early.

The friends made their goodbyes. Promised to get together soon.

*

Sarah offered to draw a hot bath for Ron prior to tucking him in. He concurred absently. When the bath was ready, she looked for him in the living room and then the bedroom. She went upstairs to the office. His was seated at his desk, his back to her, bent over his computer, his fingers flying over the keys as if in a desperate race to the finish.

"What else—what more do you want?" he growled furiously.

"Ron, honey, the bath is ready."

"I'll do it, damn you! I've got it all written down here—" He waved the small notebook wildly over his head. "It's all here. Now just let me type it out."

Nervously, Sarah approached her husband's back. Peering over his shoulder, she caught a glimpse of the rage emitted by the words on the screen.

"That should please you. Just look at it! It's great! They'll eat it up!" he cried.

He turned around to see his wife standing there.

"What are you doing there?"

"Honey, your bath—"

"Can't you see that I'm busy?" he roared.

He turned back to face the glowing screen. His head moved left to right and back again, as he looked by turns at the notes scrawled in the notebook and at the computer monitor, to which he was transcribing the half-formed story he had scribbled at the restaurant.

"This should make you happy—it's done, the first draft, that is. I'll flesh it out. I'll transform it into art. My character will be renowned as Anger made flesh. Living, breathing, incarnate Rage. They will call it a masterpiece!"

Sarah observed the heaving of her husband's shoulders in time with his inhalation and exhalation of slow and deep, lung-filling breaths.

"Ron, honey . . . I'm happy with it if you're happy. You know I love your writing."

"What the hell—" Ron swung around and glared at his wife with undisguised disgust.

"You're overwrought, babe. I don't want the bath to grow cold, and you look so tired, but if you prefer to keep working, I'll just let you be, sweetie."

"You—" Ron jumped up from the desk, knocking his chair over. "Can't you see I'm working?"

Sarah took a backward step toward the door.

"Sure, hon, I'll leave you be."

She edged toward the door, keeping her eyes on his face.

The fiery scarlet glow from the computer screen momentarily drew her attention.

A red-faced demon, a distortion of her husband, leered at her from the monitor, running its split tongue over its lips.

Stifling a scream, she turned to run out the door.

"You wanted to go downstairs, did you? Well, allow me to assist."

After he threw his wife down the stairs, Ron returned to his desk.

"Say, that was a good idea I had. I'm going to have my main character throw his wife down the stairs, breaking her neck. I've got to make it a real convincing scene. I'm up to it—I know. My work 'demonstrates an enormous outpouring of descriptive power,' according to the critic at *The Times*.

"Let's see, the man is hard at work on his computer when his sniveling wife interrupts him. I need to show how his fury builds so that the murder is inevitable by the end of the scene. This story is going to make me famous."

Programmed

"Oh, do you think it will hurt the poor baby?"

"Not at all. They'll use anesthesia."

"But cutting into the skull and everything . . ."

"Think of the freedom from wearing straps about one's head. Reality will be implanted in the individual now, rendering external apparatus obsolete."

"Yes, dear. Our child will not need to wear a monitor before his face any more, as we have done. He'll have reality in his brain."

"Well, he'll be a lucky one. Yet what would we have done if we'd had to look at the world without the benefit of a monitor before our faces? What if we'd had to make sense of everything by ourselves? There would be chaos!"

"Enola, just get down on your knees and give thanks for the Internet. I remember how it all began: first, clunky, labor-saving computing machines, and then smaller ones, used primarily for typing better, and then when they came up with games! Oh, ho! and then social media! That's when people saw the light!"

"Yes, George, there was no putting them down, especially when they were small enough to be carried in people's hands. People no longer were forced to look at the physical world—or other people, for that matter. They walked around holding their phones in front of them, looking at the world in the pictures they carried instead of looking around them."

"Glory be, Enola! People had found the Truth: Big Brother spoke to them always from the palms of their hands. Big Brother told them what was true and what was false. What the weather would be the next five days, and what was going on in China and in Chile and the Kardashian household. People could stop reading books and newspapers. They could stop asking their neighbors and teachers to explain things to them: Big Brother speaking to them from the palms of their hands was all they needed."

"George, don't forget the shopping and the games! People soon became addicted. They could not put their phones down, and every move they made was directed by the Truths told them by Big Brother."

"People stopped reading books, chapters, pages—and they telegraphed their thoughts in Twitter feeds—so their thoughts grew smaller, and they didn't need very many of them at all anymore. The eradication of individual thought is one of the greatest benefits of the Internet. A lot of people preferred sex on their phones to physical relations with other people—and talking to heads of people in their palms to talking with full-grown people in their bodies. People stopped needing people at all after a time, when they perfected virtual reality."

"Everything they needed was delivered: they didn't need to leave their homes, which was good, because they kept tripping when they walked with their phones in front of their eyes. This has been a problem with the monitors affixed in front of our faces even now, strapped around our heads. The collision warning systems have not been quite adequate to prevent people from missing their steps and falling in front of traffic or running into each other on occasion."

"The next generation will be fortunate to have Reality implanted in their brains, Enola. They will have a clear visual field, and Big Brother in their brains will tell them what they see and what it means. No one will ever have to figure anything out again, decide for themselves what is right and wrong and what to do after work, or how many kids to have. Big Brother will tell them about Reality, and they won't ever have to see and hear and learn things for themselves. And they won't even have to walk around with a monitor before their eyes. Aren't they the lucky ones?"

"Oh, George, it will be a brave new world indeed—Truth and Reality no longer debated, everyone receiving the same digital Revelation. No more arguments, wars, or literary criticism: everyone will be programmed with the same ideas. No more competitions, original ideas challenging old beliefs. There is only one Truth, and everyone will know it."

"Enola, I wonder what we will do or think or feel next?"

"George, we've recharged our circuits, and our thoughts should have been downloaded by now. I'm feeling affectionate—please bump your face monitor against mine. That was nice."

"I wonder how people managed before computers told them what to do, how to do it, when to do it, and with whom to do it?"

"Ditto. And what to think and feel. How do you think they ever figured out what to think and feel on their own?"

"Enola, let's not go there. We know we have the truth about Reality now. Let's play Catch the Peppermints."

"And then, let's buy that voice-activated computer that turns things on and off, so we don't have to push buttons and flip switches any more. They're the latest thing."

Out of This World

Red-tangerine flames leap, climb over one another. Brush-heap snaps, crackles, deploys miniscule rockets that sizzle, fizzle, pop, spraying sanguine-hued streamlets in the dark sky around the blaze in the center of the circle. Blonde girl starts, did it hit me, did it burn me, and Benny says let me look at it I'll take care of it I won't let anything happen to you. Beth Anne leans her shoulders back into Benny's chest, I like you right there, baby.

Want a hit, Joe, Laura? It's a warm night for Halloween, isn't it? Any hot dogs, marshmallows left? How's about another bottle of beer? Pass it right over. Hold it for me, babe, while I put more wood on the fire.

You'll see, Joe, Laura, out in the woods tonight, after dark, when they're out, you'll see what I've been telling you is the truth. It's friggin' *weird*. These animals, they're not normal. They *do* things.

Hey, quit it, Ben! You're not gonna scare us. We'll come along for the gag—appropriate for Halloween—we like fun as much as you two weirdos, but you're not going to scare us so easy as that, like we're sitting on our bunks at summer camp listening to ghost stories while the counselors knock on the window and go 'Whoo Whoo' to make us wet our pants.

No? Well, follow me. Let me show you.

Four old friends stand up, yawn, stretch, shuffle back to the road. I'll show you what I saw. It's creepy. It's a snake. Yeah, a couple of days ago I saw it on my hike, curled up, dead or sleeping in the morning chill. When I went out the next day the skin had been *cut,* from the head down—about four inches—not ripped not torn, but cut clean around the circumference, and the rest of the skin was still there, all the way to the tail, the only injury I could see was the missing last four inches of skin. Red meat instead of black snakeskin on the last four inches of the snake. You tell me how did that happen?

Maybe there's an apprentice serial killer honing his skills in the woods. Maybe someone dared someone to bite off the snake's head and all he could manage was to suck off the skin— *Stop it, Joe, or you'll end up by yourself tonight!* Point taken, Laur. Where'd you see it, Ben?

By the side of the road. Keep walking, geez, I thought it was closer.

Benny, I don't think we're going in the right direction. It didn't take us this long to walk from the road to the campsite when we got here. Do you see our cars?

Colossal orange orb, grinning Harvest Moon calls up formless shadows, brings forth grey blemishes, dark grey, black stains, cool whitish-grey puddles—peers down from outer space to appraise his handiwork. Parti-colored men, women, beasts, checkered trees' leaves waving madly call diabolically come here come here it's moonlight and it's Devil's Night, the earth is washed in moonglow.

Watch out—take my hand, Laura. *Guys, hurry!* Turkeys wild turkeys from the woods big flock, a dozen *running to attack us.* Come on, I don't want to tangle with insane fowl!

Two couples hasten, flee from onrushing birds. Gobble gobble gobble, foul incantation of unearthly fowl. Red, burning eyes gobble gobble. Loathsome winged beasts of destruction gobble gobble. Red eyes intent on kids' eyes, plucking them out of their heads if they can. Kids outrun the lunatic beasts, did you guys ever see birds on the attack before, I mean except for that old movie, never happens in real life.

We don't want to see the snake anymore, Ben, come back to the fire with Joe and me. Let's put the fire out and then find our cars after. I don't see the road, do you?

Reality is a grey/white/black splotch zebra-striped or jail-striped pin-striped lines down your face or clothes, discontinuous shadow and moonshine, liquefied world stirred not shaken oozing like oil, no outlines, no borders, greys melding with greys, fluid, amorphous.

Joe, I don't even see the fire anymore, Joe—don't let go of my hand, where's Beth Anne, I don't see her.

I'm here, Laura, with Benny, we're good. I can barely see you two. Funny such a big moon and everything so grey and hazy. Maybe the fire went out, that's why we can't see it. How long have we been walking? Where's the road?

Halloween—on the edge of town, where streets give way to sown fields and unturned meadows, dark, secret woods beyond. Outside the pale of streetlights, buildings, and automobiles. Good to enjoy a bonfire with friends on a frosty night. Cool, crazy Hallows' Eve lark, but how to go back now, where is the car, where is the road, where is the fire we built so red and hot and cooked hot dogs on sticks over? Only gruesome, surgically flayed snakes and attack-turkeys, nothing else but shadows minus forms, nebulous entities—*what's that?*

Beth Anne screams as Ben falls, pulling her to the ground with him. Did you step in a hole, hon, no something ran into my legs, something big, something furry. Laura and Joe sweep the lights on their phones sweep them in a circle, look for the interloper that tripped poor Ben. No, we're not hurt, just shaken, it's all right. Let's walk, but where. Grey, black, moon-pallor world. U*mm*pph! Laura lands flat on her face.

I saw it! A groundhog jumped up on her back knocked her on her face. A groundhog? I hope you didn't break your nose, honey, I'll help you up, help you make up your face if you have a shiner in the morning, Joe, Ben, where's the road, the cars, all grey, all smoke and shadow everywhere, Beth Anne hurt her knee, too.

We don't know, can't see, can't see a thing but grey patches, white shadows, a big moon with no light only misshapen shadows, not normal shadows, dreadful silhouettes. An oblivion assembled from nocturnal chasms peopled with night-things, indefinable and shapeless. Moving colors, can colors move, have agency, is that what they mean by "shades," where the hell is the road, the cars, can you see the glow of the embers? I think the fire's gone out.

Mottled vaporous biosphere, pitch black would be less equivocal than this shifting morass. Let's call for help, admit we're lost, wait to get rescued, follow dispatcher's instructions. God, no Internet reception here—no phone, just our wits, we'll be fine in the morning when we can see again, damn haze and shadows will be gone when the sun rises, only a few hours.

Joe, you're awful quiet, are you okay, yes Laura, I've just been thinking I feel as if we've walked out of the world, is this the same place we left? Don't talk crazy, Joe, we're just lost in the country, not that far from town, in the morning we'll be fine, we'll laugh it off.

Let's look for a clearing, build a fire, stay put till morning, use our cell phone lights to find a way out of the tangled woods with the creeping roots and grabbing branches, ominous shadows, we can sit around the fire, all the food and beer's back at the campsite, more in the cars, but we can't find them, or we could just go home or to the bar knock back some Jack Daniel's.

Packed-earth, tromped-down soil, who cleared this glade, a good place to build a fire. I'll get the kindling, I'll help, and I'll supply the lighter. Ben's arm around Beth Anne, Joe's around

Laura, they sit, reddened with fireglow, waiting for dawn. Red dances, pirouettes on the branches, glides across the leaves, steps en pointe across four weary faces. Red sparkles like stars on high branches of tall trees, red pokes its nose into the labyrinthine forest, red colors everything the hue of blood.

Do you see that, where the firelight is dancing, over there—it's a stone, a stone with markings, carvings, maybe a location marker, let's look, shine our lights. GOD—HORRIBLE—what *is* it, the thing in the stone, a gargoyle, an eldritch idol, graffiti?

Did it move? I tell you, it moved!

Two stones, not one—train your light here, look more of the same, more weird carvings, chiseled phantasmagoric creatures, demonic denizens of another plane. Who has done this?

The space enlarges—the cleft between the stones—the stones can't move, don't move, where is that space, what is that void, how does it grow. The black spills out, seeps into the glade. Alive, I think it's alive. Use your head, it can't be alive. Let's get out of here. We did, I knew it, we walked out of the world.

Four souls turn to fly, naught but pitch blackness on all sides of them, midnight darkness, stygian gloom, black sans fireshine, sans moonpallor, sans . . . sans anything but unseen, hideous things in a gloomy gulf. Black below, black above, black all around. Black, slurping, subsuming, absorbing them into an imploding abyss.

The Great Beyond

Holiday Shopping

The approach of the holidays is inevitably preceded by a season of shopping. Thus, I had accumulated two or three armfuls of the most adorable sequined dresses, luxe knit pullovers, flirty skirts that fluttered above the knee, and rhinestone-trimmed cardigans, which I was carrying toward the fitting room at the rear of a delicious store known as Paradise, gaily contemplating how I would have to plan sufficient theater dates and dinners in fine restaurants (maybe I would even throw a party) to provide the necessary opportunities for the wearing of these heavenly ensembles—whose magic could transform a nondescript female into an enchanted princess, a glamorous runway model, a succulent debutante. Verily, the Holiday Season is the most wonderful time of the year—for decadently wallowing in bling. Rose gold satin, glitter pumps, lacquered evening bags . . . oh, my! I placed my hand upon my heart. Each time I advanced with my precious burden of velvet and lace, a salesperson intercepted my progress, saying, "Allow me to take these to the fitting room for you, Mademoiselle, they are *très magnifique! Certainement,* you have exquisite taste."

My shopping habit is to thoroughly survey all the baubles proffered in couturier fashion houses, such as this bewitching boutique, ere I disrobe down to my unmentionables and commence the Trying On of the garments. That being said, I passed a goodly span of time in the fitting room, the hooks on the walls of which were threatening to abdicate from the lavender-painted particle board with the weight of all the fashions I had selected hanging upon them. Whoever said it was the clothes that make the man, in this case woman, knew whereof he spoke. In the mirror I beheld an *Angel*—my old self transfigured through the powers of an enchanting frock. Regarding me from the silvered glass was She Who I Wish to Be! I cracked the louvered door and poked my nose out.

"Excuse me, miss," I called. "Excuse me," a little louder the second time. I was hoping that the helpful salesperson could find me a smaller size in the pewter-colored metallic box-pleated mini skirt. "Hello, is anyone there?"

I exited my cubicle and stood in the little vestibule with its three-way mirrors and multiple closed louvered doors, which were circled like wagons around me. "Is anyone else in here?" I was answered by silence. The fine hairs on the back of my neck alerted me that this peculiar Silence was aggressive, an absence of sound demanding notice.

I moved past the three Me's who were preening in the mirrors, bedecked in a dusty-rose pink, rhinestone-covered wrap dress (à la Furstenberg) and champagne satin pumps with darling pink bows on their heels, and I pulled aside the curtain that separated the dressing room alcove from the shopping area of this delectable retail Cloud Nine.

It wasn't there!

—the store!—

It really wasn't there!

Only endless space, a lavender-hued eternity swirling in undulating nothingness. A strange luminescence replacing time and space and form. A soundless void of arcane mystery.

The walls of the shop were floating at strange angles, suspended in the ether, and drifting away to the left and to the right. I looked down at the floor, which had dropped aeons below me. I stepped back into the chamber, lest I fall off the edge of the floor and into the bottomless expanse below. Far away above, floating aimlessly, were the erstwhile ceiling of the store and the chandelier that used to hang from it. The promised land of couture, now a dressing room in an infinite vacuum.

The boutique had a little while ago seemed to me to be a morsel of heaven, heaven a fancy-dress ball where gentlemen and ladies are handsome, fascinating, and blissful all the time.

Now the dressing room was the totality of existence— comprised of myself and a heap of breathtaking off-the-rack finery tossed upon a tufted ottoman, and bounded by mirrors on every side reflecting the images reflected by the other mirrors. And nowhere to go in these costly habiliments, and no one to compliment me on how beautiful I look when I wear them.

Poor Winona

"It's all my fault. I killed you," Jessica sobbed.

Curled up into a fetal position on her bed, she smashed her face into the pillow, soaking it with her tears.

"Oh, Winona, I shouldn't have gone to visit Cheryl in Detroit and left you all alone over the weekend while I was playing progressive slots. I love you so much—and, yet, *I let you starve to death!*"

The overstuffed eyelet comforter was growing wrinkled with the heaving of her grief-wracked body, and the precision hospital corners of the linens were all at sixes-and-sevens.

"Oh, Winona, sweet, pretty goldfish, *I killed you!*"

Jessica went on this way for quite some time, and then she flushed Winona down the toilet.

"Our Father, who art . . . or maybe a Hail Mary would be more appropriate. Should I pray to St. Francis? He loves animals

. . . Oh, poor Winona!"

As one might expect, Jessica had no appetite all the rest of the day. She was not a drinker, or she would have gotten soused. She just cried herself to sleep instead, swathed in remorse for murdering her best friend through selfish neglect.

The next thing she knew, she was snorkeling in Lake Huron— and looking quite fetching in a sleek rubber outfit, complete with matching flippers and goggles. She was blowing happy bubbles from the tube in her mouth and marveling at the corpses of wrecked ships and the oodles of waving corals in psychedelic colors, like lime green, fluorescent orange, and hot pink (pink was her favorite color—and it was Winona's, too!).

Suddenly there was a great turbulence in the water. The dark green fluid roiled, pushing her down as she strove to reach the surface. She swam with all her might, trying to rise to the top, kicking her finned feet harder and harder, her heart pounding with the strenuous labor, running out of air, trying to ration her breaths. She thought she was going to die!

But then a great golden creature came rushing to her in the water. It was huge, and it was getting bigger as it moved straight at her.

As it drew near, Jessica could see its iridescent golden scales and the malevolent gleam of its golden, bulging eyes—

"Winona! Winona—you're alive!"

Jessica was overcome with joy—until Winona—grown gigantic— opened her garage-door-size mouth, baring two rows of razor-like teeth. The jaws opened wider—and Jessica fell in . . .

She woke up screaming, waving her arms as if she were treading water. Only after a harrowing minute or two did she realize that she was safe in her (tousled) bed.

"It was only a dream," she murmured, "Poor, Winona. You're dead. I killed you. I didn't mean to . . . it was an accident . . . I loved you!"

She rose from her bed, put her pink slippers on, and trudged into the kitchen. She boiled a cup of water in the microwave, poured in a spoonful of Maxwell House Instant Coffee, and sat down at the Formica table, where the newspaper was open to the front page. She looked at the headline:

"Oh, my Lord!" she exclaimed, as she read about the Flint water crisis. She had been drinking water contaminated with lead, showering with it—and—and—she had put it into Winona's fish bowl! She had even flushed Winona into poisonous streams.

"All this time, unbeknown to her, how darling Winona must have been suffering in silence! If only I had learned to read bubbles . . ." Jessica blamed herself.

Unfortunately, the only fish language she knew was that upside-down equals dead. What signs of Winona's distress had she failed to see in time?

Despite her grief at the loss of her significant other, Jessica had to pull herself together to go to work. She bathed—with bottled water—and scrubbed her face clean, erasing the tearstains and reddening the skin of her already florid complexion. She pulled her dishwater-blonde hair back into a severe bun, put on a pink sundress and Birkenstocks, and picked up her Mary Kay case. Steeling herself, she went out the door to ply her trade.

She walked door to door through her neighborhood in Flint, knocking on doors, and, when the doors were closed in her face, she left brochures at all the apartments in all the apartment buildings for several blocks. At the end of six hours she had sold a lipstick and a concealer, to an elderly lady who kept asking, "Are you sure you're all right, dear?" She tried hard to focus on her dream—acquiring a pink Cadillac by tapping the innate power of the salesmanship she had learned that she possessed, when she had attended the Mary Kay Seminar held at the Holiday Inn in Detroit two years before. Whenever thoughts of poor Winona—and her own guilt—rose in her mind, Jessica tried to envision herself driving a pink Cadillac: cruising right past the Greektown Casino in Detroit, luxuriating as dozens of pedestrians and bus-riders turned their heads, green with envy of the youngish woman at the wheel of a pink Cadillac! *But all see could see was a dead Winona floating upside down in the driver's seat.*

Her feet were sore, and recurrent habitual thoughts that it was time to feed Winona were intruding themselves upon her tired mind, crowding out the rosy visions of pink Cadillacs, and so she returned to her apartment. She sank heavily into the unsprung futon, which had seen better days, and thought that she had better eat—to keep her strength up, lest she pine away in guilt and grief. It would serve her right, though, God knows. Possessing no heart for cooking a box of macaroni and cheese, she just poured a glass of milk, took a handful of Oreos from an open package on the counter, and returned to the futon, where she dunked her cookies in the milk, making a little mess of it— ordinarily she was a tidy housekeeper—because her dunking and mastication were attended by bouts of tearfulness, which resulted in soggy crumbs and splashes upon the furniture. Experiencing the anhedonia that usually accompanies grief, Jessica rinsed her glass and left it unwashed (oh, what a sign of her coming unstrung—for she truly took pride in good housekeeping!) in the sink, and went to bed, throwing her clothes upon the floor in an extravagant gesture of misery.

She found herself on the H.M.S. Titanic. *She felt claustrophobic: on the deck of the streamer-strewn vessel, which was filled with somber ladies and gentlemen in evening dress and furs, pointing their fingers at a huge block of ice on the horizon. Forlorn, she leaned over the rail, letting her tears fall into the ocean, as she thought of Winona, who by this time would have made her way into the deep. Yes, a maritime burial was consistent with the dignity of the passing of an aquatic creature, albeit a sweet little goldfish named Winona.*

Suddenly the ship's orchestra began playing "Nearer My God to Thee," and the air was filled with screams of terror—for the ship was rolling on the great swells, tossed forward and aft, left and right (Jessica couldn't remember the proper maritime lingo), as if she would roll over and capsize. The front end of the ship lifted up into the air as gargantuan waves rose up—right in front of her—where there had been picturesque ripples only moments before. Whitecaps rose like mountains, and the spray drenched all the passengers on the upper decks. Jessica was clinging to the rail for dear life when out from the deep swam a gigantic gold fish—a goldfish!—Winona, a giant Winona now! Winona opened a fanged brontosaurus-sized mouth and swam straight at Jessica, opening her mouth even wider—!

She awoke, drenched in a cold sweat.

"I deserve to suffer from nightmares," she sighed, "for I killed my poor Winona."

Unable to pull herself together to tread the pavement, working toward her pink Cadillac, she pulled her eyelet comforter from the bed, curled up in it on the futon, and turned on the TV. *The Price is Right* was ending, and the afternoon movie was beginning. She closed her eyes, leaning her head against the back of the futon, as she waited for the series of sponsors' messages to end.

When she heard the opening bars of *Jaws* she screamed, clicking off the television.

"I'm a murderess—and my conscience will not let me ever know happiness again!"

She swallowed three Tylenol P.M. and returned to her bed, seeking refuge from her pain in sleep. She did not even care if they found her dead of an overdose: she couldn't live with her grief and her guilt anymore. She pulled the eyelet comforter (by this time sadly in need of laundering) around her as a cocoon and willed the drug to take effect.

Instead of the oblivion she craved, she found herself sunning on the rock-strewn sand of the Lake Huron beach. Clad in a revealing pink bikini, she stretched out, tanned and lovely. As she was getting quite hot in the noonday sun, she decided to go wading in the surf. Through the cool, green-blue water she could see her toes and the rounded stones beneath her feet, and she bent to pick up a stone. She would see if she still had the knack for skipping stones on the water. This was going to be a nice dream. But as she rose, stone in hand, she cried out:

"Winona!"

Her monstrous deceased friend was coming toward her, the Jaws *music playing in the wind.*

She leapt from her bed, screaming. "Oh, God, is there no surcease from my sorrow?" she sobbed, remembering Poe, for she had memorized "The Raven" for her senior English class in high school. She thought that the narrator must have loved Lenore as she had loved Winona.

Jessica dragged herself to the window and looked wistfully upon the stormy tableau of Flint, Michigan, bathed in the lavender glow of twilight and interspersed with lightning strikes. *It certainly does look different in this light,* she mused, *my boring old hometown turned surreal.* She dabbed her eyes and thought, *I'll take a walk out there. It will do me some good.*

And so she retrieved her mackintosh from the closet and, picking up her keys from the Formica kitchen table, went to her door. Unfastening the chain, she pulled the door open—and ran smack into an invisible wall.

"What the—?"

First she touched the small bump on her forehead—and then she reached out to touch the glass wall beyond the door.

"I'm closed in—in glass!" she exclaimed.

Returning to the window, she thought she might attempt to exit her apartment by the fire escape—but when she raised the sash and put out her hand, she felt a glass wall between herself and the mysteriously luminous sky.

"How do I get out?" she cried, although there was no one to hear her wailing. "I'll never earn a pink Cadillac! I'll starve if I can't even get to the store!

"Is this how you felt in the fishbowl, Winona?"

She sobbed—and then she began to laugh.

After three weeks she starved to death in her doorway. The following day her landlord found her when he came to inquire about her missing rent check.

Lunar Mission

Hand-in-hand round golden rings, maidens skip,
Pink lunar dust wafts up while they keep time.
With hands-across and half-poussette, they clip;
And boldly troubadours romances rhyme
With woodwind airs and thrums of lyre strings,
While swains slay dragons in the starry sky,
Embarked on quests to fetch down Saturn's rings.
Pusses-in-Boots and Ulthar cats leap nigh
To Venus, Jupiter, and warlike Mars,
Where sightless mole-men tunnel catacombs—
Spyholes—so bright blue whales may see the stars—
And Mother Goose has tea with Sherlock Holmes.
Whene'er I visit the back side of the moon,
I planet-hop, fly in my mind's balloon;
And, yet (declare dull mortals made of clay)
The dark side of the moon is cold and grey.

Dolly

A faux-wool rayon blend blanket—blue or green, I think—is fluttering in the wind. I do not feel a wind, but I see that the blanket is fluttering. It is hanging, as if on a clothesline, but there is no clothesline, nor anything else upon which my blanket could have hung itself; at least I cannot see anything.

I am lying, with my eyes open, in a twin bed. I see myself looking at the blanket. There is just me in the bed and the blanket. There are no roof or walls, but there is a floor—wood planks, it looks like, probably made of contact paper. Nothing more.

Then the rain starts, thunder and lightning, getting me, the bed, and the blanket wet.

Next thing I know, I am being awakened for breakfast. I see myself sitting at a table—a kitchen sort of table, in a kitchen, a white plate before me, nothing on it. There is a lady guest in the house. We are going to lunch. I am to wear a blue dress.

I am in the narrow bed again. It is flat and hard. There is a light covering over my body. It is dark now. No sounds. A black and silent nothingness, until—

I find myself in a red satin ball gown, stiff pleats of gold-embroidered crimson encircling my form, too long for me, my feet cannot touch the ground. I am held up off the floor by the skirt. My hair is piled on top of my head. I am going to a ball. There is to be a prince with whom I am to fall in love. Elbow-length white gloves cover my arms.

The next thing I know I am clad in dungarees, plaid shirt, and a faun-colored ten-gallon hat over my golden locks, and I am sitting atop a tan Palomino. A noiseless, motionless golden retriever sits next to the horse and me.

I am lying in my small, hard bed, in floral flannel pajamas, beneath a square of light cotton. It is very dark. I cannot see the sky, nor the stars, nor the sun. I have not heard a noise for what seems like a very long time, although I have lain with my eyes and ears open. I think that now a roof and walls close me in.

It is teeth that I see next, two massive rows of sharp, white-yellow teeth, covered with slick, wet liquid, in a pink mouth. They sink into my body, marring its smooth surface, shrouding me in pink tongue and gums. I lose an arm. Then my hair is chewed to shreds, and a big patch is pulled out in back and sticks in the sharp teeth. Fangs impale my face—one in front and one behind. My flannel pajamas are a soggy, smelly mess.

I lie now amid a heap of decaying remnants of food, flesh that has liquefied and is being feasted upon by legions of flies whose mouths smack of sugar. Bottles, cans, crushed pizza box-es, and soiled disposable diapers compress into myself.

Anon comes a landslide of refuse. A mountain falling upon the mountain that is my grave. The flies rise up, a buzzing black cloud, as the cataract of trash descends upon me, and then the flies return.

A ridge of rough, razor steel, as thick as my waist, cleaves the mount of rubbish and cleaves my body in two. We are lifted up on a load of putrid materials, high into the sky, and then allowed to fall from the lofty heights to end up once more upon the pile of rubbish. Then raised and dropped again, onto a moving piece of rubber, jostled among pieces of glass and plastic laundry de-tergent containers, sorted into various groups according to what we are made of.

By hellfire I am melted, shapeless putty—my top half; I do not know what has become of my nether parts—in an iron caul-dron that any devil would be proud to possess. Then I am squashed so hard I think I shall have been obliterated, but when the steel that encases me is moved away, I see that I have be-come a round basin, a pink round basin.

From me a dog drinks water, slobbering, splashing water with each lap, wetting the floor with his snorting.

A Much-Needed Rest

Helena wilted in the cane chair in her office. Her body was draped over it—her head lolling over the back of the chair, her arms limply depending from the arms of the chair, her legs splayed to the sides of the chair. She realized that her posture was not very ladylike, but—well, she was simply too exhausted to support herself in an upright position at this time, thank you. On how many ends can one burn a candle, she mused, too tired to think about anything but her fatigue. *I guess I could not have maintained such momentum forever,* she thought. *I've simply got to crash now.* Thankfully, she had already packed her bags before the crisis had come.

She stirred herself to a sitting position when she heard a knock at the door. The knock came a second time, more insistent. "I'm coming," she called, and got to her feet. She walked to the door and opened it.

"I'm here to take you to the airport," the driver said.

Helena gestured toward her luggage, and the man picked up her suitcases and carried them to the car. After he stowed them in the trunk, he held the door for her. When she had settled into her seat and they were under way, he asked,

"Business or pleasure?"

"A much-needed rest," she answered. Cold white sheets, freshly pressed and tucked into the mattress of a four-poster in a one-time plantation home, hijacked her thoughts. The bed to which she was headed was in an upper room, with a balcony facing the sea, in a pillared mansion on a privately owned island, a hundred miles from Tahiti. She was to be the only guest, for it was, blessedly, the off-season. She would check in and then sleep for a day or two—perhaps three!—and then, perhaps, she would enjoy the white sands and blue water of the South Pacific.

Her life had been a struggle. She had fled an abusive home as a teenager, lived on charity, slept on friends' sofas, and earned two college degrees, by a combination of scholarships and working a multitude of odd jobs. She had only in the last year realized success in her career, and the exhaustion had set in, which is why she found herself on her way to what used to be known as "a rest cure." When she had received an advertisement in the mail for this luxurious vacation destination, she had seized the opportunity. She would return home ready to embrace her new life.

It was torture, the airport lines, the security checkpoints. During the ordeal she uttered as few words as possible, not wanting to risk starting a conversation with anyone. At last she took her seat by the window of the three-quarters-filled plane. She reclined her seat, just a little, for she knew that she would be infringing upon the space of the person behind her if she put it back all the way. She placed her sleep mask on her head and curled her body against the window, and was out before the flight attendant finished her safety spiel. The attendant nudged her shoulder when it was time to prepare for landing at the Tahiti airport.

Helena found herself repeating the pre-flight obstacle course, with the addition of a cursory interview at the customs window. She followed the signs to the luggage carousel, and there she spotted the cream-colored-linen-suited driver bearing a card printed in thick black letters: *Helena Adams*. Helena waved to her driver, who hastened to retrieve her bags. Once inside the comfortable car, she laid her head upon the back of the seat and enjoyed the silent ride to the waterfront.

"Here you are, mademoiselle," the man said (Helena had only just noticed that he was good-looking). "The plane that will convey you to the island is over there." She turned her head to look where he was pointing.

Two hours later the propeller plane was landing on the runway of her island. A cream-colored sedan rolled up right next to the plane, and a woman in a smart white suit emerged from it to say,

"Mademoiselle Adams, I am Marie. Allow me to welcome you to your private island. Gaston has already moved your luggage into the car, and so, if you please, I will drive you to the house."

Helena looked appreciatively upon the great expanse of green lawn through which the half-mile drive wound a leisurely path to the house. Soon the august mansion rose up before the front window of the car, preceded by an acre of red flowers and large, leafy shrubs. Marie parked the car and opened the door for Helena, who ascended the twenty steps of the porch.

Planks of whitewashed hardwood formed the floor and ceiling of the porch. Great wrought-iron chandeliers hung from the rafters at regular intervals. Helena pushed open the imposing double doors with frosted glass panels and was pleased with the deep crimson carpeting and ornately carved mahogany tables of the foyer.

"Mademoiselle Adams," a woman in a white silk dress said as she crossed the room toward Helena, "welcome. I am Annette. How was your journey? Please accompany me to the desk, where we will complete your registration, so that your stay with us may begin."

Helena signed her name where indicated, provided her passport and her credit card, and said that she'd like to go to her room immediately. Oh, and could she have a cup of chamomile tea? And she was soon in her own room.

The first thing she did was to place the *Do Not Disturb* sign on the door. And then she removed her clothes, laid them across the back of a chair, and got into her bed, the sheets of which were every bit as crisp and cool and white as she had dreamed of. And, listening to the wind and the waves, she fell asleep before dark.

She awoke to the crashing of glass. The French doors of her balcony had blown open, and shards of glass were flying in every direction. The diaphanous curtains were blowing crazily in and out of the doorway. Rain was saturating the Delft-blue carpet and the white cotton sheets of her bed.

She leapt from the bed and heard the beastly howling of the wind. The French doors were blowing open and shut and open again. Helena fought the storm inside her room to close the doors and latch them, and she pushed the vanity in front of them to hold them shut. And then she pulled on some sweat pants and a T-shirt and opened her door to look out into the hall.

"Annette! Marie! Gaston! Is anybody there?" she called. The screaming of the wind was her only answer. She called once more and, receiving no reply, ventured into the long white hall of many closed doors and thick red carpet. As she walked the rolling halls, she felt the house rocking as a boat on a livid ocean.

"Annette! Marie! Gaston! Where is everyone? What is going on?" she called, making an effort to maintain her balance when the thick walls about her shuddered.

Clinging to the rail, she descended the swaying stairs into the red and mahogany lobby. "Hello, Marie! Annette! Gaston! What is it? Answer me!" she cried. The ocean roared in response and entered in through the front door, sending the round mahogany table with the urn of red flowers floating toward the reception desk.

Helena pulled herself up on the rail, back to the second floor. She ran the length of the hall, trying every door to find a passage to the attic or the roof. Finding every door but the door of her own room locked, she retreated to her former haven. She shut the door and locked it; then she rolled up the bedclothes and towels and pushed them up to the bottoms of the hall and balcony doors. She tried to call for help on the French phone on the night table, but the line was dead.

I hope this storm ends before the water gets in here, she thought. She returned to the bed, now a bare mattress, where once had been crisp, cool white sheets and an ivory silk comforter, now the materials of her dike. Her gaze was fixed at the bottom of the door; she listened to the hammering of the rain against the glass of the French doors and on the white planks of the walls. She no longer knew whether the darkness outside her window was the night or the storm, what time of day it was.

She knew how her story would end when she saw the water coming in through the wadded linens at the bottom of the hall door. She removed the vanity and the linens from the French doors of the balcony, whereupon the doors crashed open and the storm assailed her body with thousands of needle-sharp raindrops. Fighting the hundred-mile-per-hour winds, she clawed her way out onto the balcony. She could see nothing, the water stinging her eyes when she tried. She found herself in the midst of a living, swirling, watery hell. It required all her strength, but she climbed up on the wrought-iron railing and pushed herself into the maelstrom.

*

Back in New York, under the rubric of "breaking news," the newscasters were talking of her disappearance. A young American, who had recently made a name for herself and had gone off for a vacation in the vicinity of Tahiti, had boarded a plane for a remote island. Neither plane nor pilot nor Helena had been heard of since. No one was sure exactly which island had been her destination. It had been a beautiful day, the yellow sun shining in a blue sky that had not even a single cloud. Yet the plane and the people in it had seemed to vanish from the face of the earth. Aviation investigators had converged in the waters off Tahiti. The news team would keep viewers posted with the latest information as it surfaced.

Cataclysm

That bird—it just swooped down from the sky—came straight for me! Ariel watched the vulture alight upon the peaked roof of an abandoned farmhouse across the street, where it assumed a dignified stance beside two of its brethren, who had already perched there. Ariel often sighted wild turkeys and hawks, even the occasional bat, on her daily walks, but she had never seen a vulture before. *Make that a trio of vultures (one of which swooped at me) settled primly in single file upon the roof of a dilapidated house.* She added this sign to the lengthening list of dismal portents she had encountered that morning. *Vultures are attracted by carrion!* she thought, sensing the imminent approach of an unnamable catastrophe.

The cataclysm took place on the Autumnal Equinox.

It had been a deceptively paradisiacal, ninety-degree day: the sun had shone a bright yellow in a bold blue sky, and Ariel, who had always thrived out of doors, had left the house at dawn—to spend the entire Last Day of Summer outside. And, yet, had her neighbors been looking out of their windows instead of slumbering in their beds, they might have observed Ariel still rambling past their homes, long after nightfall, pacing the length of the darkened street and exhibiting a marked reluctance to go inside. At ten o'clock she still had not entered her house; rather, she could have been found sitting comfortably, with her feet tucked up beneath her, among the cushions on the white wrought-iron settee on her front porch, savoring the balmy night air and contemplating the deeply onyx sky embedded with glinting stars. She could not have brought herself to part with a single moment of summer.

At the same time, though, she had been studying a vanguard of black clouds. She had been able, but only just barely, to distinguish black clouds from blacker sky, by the dingy grey light the Equinox moon.

Ariel's reluctance to go into the house was a direct result of the meteorologist's forecast. Early that morning—right on television—the Channel 6 *Daybreak NewsRoom* weather woman had prophesied the dreaded End of Summer. *Much! Too! Early*! Ariel inwardly protested. Typically, the season declined gradually; but this time the meteorologist had forecast a tremendous storm, a storm that would plunge the mercury in the thermometers for the foreseeable future—the nights would be cold—and frost would soon follow. Ariel's paradisiacal Summerland was becoming a wintry Wasteland—her time in the sun was nearly up! The End of Summer was always, for Ariel, a catastrophe. She may have been afflicted by what some people brush off as Seasonal Affective Disorder, but for Ariel it was a much more intimate thing—her love of summer, that is. Ariel was, in fact, grieving for the end of her Paradise, her Season in the Sun, her daily walks under a blue sky.

All that morning Ariel had been aware that something untoward was looming: for in the course of her customary daybreak walk she had noted a number of strange and inexplicable omens of a dire nature. First, as she had exited her house to begin her walk, Ariel had observed both a pair of doves in her front yard *and* a pair of hawks—two pairs of iconic fowl signifying the opposing dynamics of peace and war—roosting on her fence, against odds nearly as impossible as two opposites fixed in the same place at the same time. The second iniquitous circumstance had occurred in the woods, where Ariel had spotted a woodpecker industriously plying his avian trade. In the past, whenever she had chanced to hear one of the crimson birds at work, all her efforts to locate the fowl among the cloaking boughs had proved fruitless; but on that inauspicious morning she had plainly observed the crested red fowl hammering its beak into the knotty trunk of an ancient oak. And, as Ariel had watched, the bird had momentarily suspended its hammering and had brazenly established eye contact with her.

Certainly, the most hideous and appalling of the ineffable events of the morning was the sight that had accosted her when she had nearly completed her walk: a bowl of bright red blood! The vessel in question had been the rib cage of what had been an opossum—she had been able to tell that by the ragged remnants of its bestial face, which, save for the grisly skeleton, were all that was left of the poor creature. The skin was gone. The heart, lungs, intestines—all the organs—were gone. The rib cage had persisted, becoming a vessel for the animal's lifeblood—a bowl of bright red blood. The fluid had not clotted. Neither was it dark. It was fresh, bright red blood. Ariel, pausing briefly to contemplate the gruesome *memento mori*, had been glad that she had not stepped in it.

When she had resumed her walk, it had seemed to Ariel that the centuries-old trees that lined both sides of the street had closed ranks—formed a barricade against the morning sunlight or some other inscrutable foe. Ariel had even witnessed the *nervous shuddering* of their leaves, when hundreds of coal-black crows had arisen from their hiding places among the branches—all, at the same time, crazily chittering to one another in some obscene language as they flew skyward. It had not been long after that when she had chanced upon the three vultures.

In light of this unnerving sequence of ominous events, the dismal prophecy croaked by the forecaster on *Daybreak News-Room* had assumed a direr aspect. As Ariel had pedaled her bicycle in the afternoon—perhaps for the last time of the year—she had discovered that her formerly carefree summery joy had withered into a meaner, sourer, sort of pleasure, best approximated by the gastronomical experience of a condemned man as he sits down to a final meal, at a table laid with his preferred dishes.

When, at midnight, a chilling Arctic wind crept in, Ariel relinquished her sad vigil, dejectedly entered her home, and resigned herself to beginning the eight- or nine-month wait for another summer. When the expected storm developed, all the blinking stars were blotted out—snuffed out, one by one—by monstrous black clouds piled atop one another, black shape upon black shape in a black void where heaven should have been.

*

A violent discharge of thunder caused Ariel to leap from her bed, in which she had been dreaming fitfully of summer's return. *Bam! Bam!*—flying branches, ripped from a tree by the wind, assailed the roof and the walls of her house. *Thrum! Thrum!*—the wind collided recklessly with the walls, snuffled up under the siding and the eaves, caused thermometers and outside light fixtures to shift their positions, abraded the sides of the house, and ruffled the shingles, separating some of them from the roof. The racket created by the driving rain upon the roof directly above her bed made it seem as if the whole house were under siege. *Kaboom!*—a riotous clatter followed a blinding flash of yellow-white light that set the night sky ablaze beyond the sheer white curtains of the bedroom window. *Crack!*—deafening thunder and disorienting lightning strobe-lit the night, creating a macabre discothèque aesthetic. *Whooshhh!*—horizontally driven, sheeting rain unremittingly pounded the house. Realizing that it was just the storm that had frightened her, Ariel rubbed her eyes, and returned to bed.

An hour later she was awakened again—the night-storm was

just too noisy for sleeping. She moved to the bow window and parted the curtains to look at the road. Headlights illumined the heavy rain that was afflicting the motorists, most of whom were undoubtedly wishing they had remained at home. Water sprayed up from the wheels of the cars.

The malign meteorologist (the one who had predicted an atypically sudden end to summer—the wicked prognostication that had so distressed Ariel all day) had explained the weather anomaly as the result the clashing of three monstrous weather systems—a tropical heat wave from the hurricane-ridden Caribbean, a mighty blast from the Antarctic Ocean, and a blizzard-bringing polar front from the Arctic Circle crawling southward over Canada—and she had warned her viewers to take precautions, to secure lawn ornaments and furniture, to stock up on necessaries in the likely event of power outages. For several decades now a slight warming of the earth's waters had augmented both the number and the severity of the storms around the globe—but, even taking that into consideration, the meteorologist had cautioned that this storm would be fearsome. The epicenter of the storm would be the middle of Lake Erie, on whose shore Ariel's two-story Cape Cod house was located, four and a half miles from the nuclear power plant; but the storm would engulf most of North America and the Arctic Circle.

When she heard the sound of glass breaking below, Ariel flew down the stairs and found the French doors, which opened from the kitchen onto the patio, hanging limply from their splintered door frames, shards of glass covering the kitchen tiles. Ariel swept up the deadly glass and then tacked a blanket over the empty door frame. Fiery red light pulsed through the window above the sink, and above the cacophony of the tempest came the wailing of sirens, as fire engines and ambulances sped down the road. Ariel gathered flashlights and candles.

When a massive maple tree crashed on top of the house next door to hers, the impact shook her own house as well, toppling a curio cabinet that held her porcelain figurines, spraying more glass. Ariel opened the side door, thinking to run to the aid of her neighbors, but a blast of wind drove her back inside. She attempted the front door—she could not get out that way, either, for the wild squall forced the door closed in her face. And then a great jolt knocked her from her feet, knocked most of the furniture over, and knocked a vase off of a shelf, which landed on her head. Ariel never saw the volcanic inferno that erupted from the cooling stack of the nuclear power plant. The flames leapt high into the night sky.

When she came to, Ariel found herself unable to rise, pinned to the floor by debris. But, more than the rubble, some force was holding her fast to the floor. She struggled, pulled herself up—clawed the upholstery of the overturned sofa—raised herself to a kneeling position. By this means she crept laboriously to the window, dragging her body along the overturned furnishings— heaved herself up to the sill—looked out the window.

She gasped when the stars and the moon whizzed by the window, speeding faster than the cars would have flown down the street on a sunny day. Clouds raced by the window, too, blurs more than conglomerations of dust and water droplets. *Could it be that her house was flying through the air?* A moment later she could see nothing beyond the window but an unrelieved gloom.

With a tremendous clamor the house . . . *burst!* The walls of the house flew outward—careened in every direction—and the ceiling soared upward, while the floor dropped from under her feet, hurtling into the vacant abyss. Ariel found herself plunging through stygian emptiness, into eternal Oblivion, conscious that she was dissolving, that the cells and subatomic particles that had been her were merging into the nothingness; and her final, ago-nizing thought was regret for the sudden, cruel loss of a glorious summer and no more summers after that.

Till Death Reunite Us

The sun had almost finished setting, and only the faint glow from the nether regions below the horizon provided a meager relief from the darkness. Liquid black was washing over the mounds and monuments of the deserted cemetery. Not entirely deserted, though, for upon a freshly filled grave, of too recent an appearance even to be marked by a headstone, a girl in a black dress was kneeling. The girl did not know that it was night.

Anne had brought flowers to her grandma's grave after the funeral lunch. Well, if you can call a cup of coffee—half a cup of coffee—lunch. She had no desire for food. Nor for anything else. Anne felt herself a void within an infinite void, a world of emp-tiness, of that which was not to be, her only grounding being her fingers clawing the turf, her black-stockinged legs pushing into the moist, new-turned earth. She pressed her knees—hard—into the dirt of the grave, for that was as close as she would ever be to her grandmother again.

Her father had died of a drug overdose, and her mother had left to find herself before she was two. Grandma Nellie had raised her and had been all-in-all to her. Anne was always pleas-ant and polite, but she was also very reclusive and had difficulty getting close to people other than her grandmother. She loved to read; in fact, when she was not helping her grandmother around the house, Anne was content to live inside the pages of her books (she loved Jane Austen) or taking long walks in the wooded park. She had never felt alone.

This day, however, for the first time, she knew loneliness; and, although she had always been possessed of a very good vocabulary, she had only just learned the meaning of "bereft"—how all your insides are ripped out of you, how you are now an empty carcass. She had loved her grandmother, and her grandmother had loved her more than life itself and had not wanted to leave her behind, but she had been obliged.

Anne was to start her freshman year at the university the next week. Nellie had been so proud of her. She could not imagine doing that now. Why should she? If we all die anyway, what does it matter what we do? *Oh, Grandma, I love you so much. Don't leave me. Take me with you.* She bent her head down to her knees and wept.

She started when she felt the delicate caress of soft fur on her muddy knee, where she had worn a ragged hole in her stocking. Raising herself to a sitting position, she saw that a white cat was snuggling against her leg. Rubbing her red-rimmed and swollen eyes with her dirty fingers, she gazed mutely at the strange interloper in her grief. The cat had rough white hair; his right ear was missing a portion, and his tail the tip. As she looked upon the white feline, he placed his front paws on her forearm and nuzzled her hand. Benumbed, she had to struggle against the inertia of her grief even to acknowledge the creature—and then, tormented by her sorrow, she snatched the scrawny cat to her breast and wept. For a very long time she sobbed; and in her arms the cat, wetted with her tears, remained still. At length she quietened, the heaving of her shoulders slowed, and her tears became fewer. She released the cat, and the cat curled up in her lap.

Twilit diamond points of light in the sky and the icy damp of the dew condensing upon the earthen coverlet of her grandmother's resting place combined to persuade Anne that it was time to go home. She gently moved the cat from her lap, kissing the top of his head, and rose to her feet. She made some ineffectual movements to brush the dirt from her clothing, and then she turned to look for the cat, thinking that perhaps he was homeless and should come home with her. But he was gone. Saddened that her little friend had disappeared, Anne also felt a peace she knew that his love had imparted to her, and all her life she would cherish the brief time when their paths had crossed upon her grandmother's grave.

*

Fierce gusts did their best to blow the hood from her head, but Anne determinedly held it in place with her left hand, while with her right she clung to her tote bag, heavy with textbooks. The driving storm needled her face without pity. Although there was only a grey sky, she wore her sunglasses to shield her eyes from the blasts of ice and snow. She trudged, lifting her booted feet high and putting them down again in the snow, which was already drifting over her ankles. She had only one more class this afternoon, Introduction to British Literature, and she was eager to discuss the adventures of Sir Gawain. She had found that she could lose herself in her schoolwork and avoid the clutches of despair.

As she rounded the corner of a red-brick building that was next door to the halls of the Department of English, a powerful blow to her jaw sent her flying to the pavement. Anne tried to clear her blurry brain and attempted to rise, but a man in black sweats and a ski mask grabbed her elbow. Thinking, *This is how I died,* Anne gathered herself to make her last stand when the man suddenly let go of her arm and screamed.

She looked up and saw that her assailant's mask was covered in gore, blood streaming from the holes that were made for seeing out of it. The snow beneath the man's feet was red now, and the man fell to his knees, still screaming the same scream. Anne dialed 911 on her phone as she pulled herself up, hugging the brick wall. Then she saw the white cat with the damaged ear. His face was slick with blood clotting from the cold. Their eyes met in mutual understanding.

Hearing the wail of sirens, Anne turned her head to the street, still hugging the wall, fearing a renewal of the attack. Two policemen came running, their guns drawn. Anne told them her story and pointed to where the cat had been. He was nowhere to be seen. The red snow indicated where he had been.

*

Anne finished her degree and continued on to graduate school. She became an English teacher so that she never had to leave school. Her students, who called her "Professor Anne," loved her for her passion for literature. She never married, happy to make a place for herself among the books that had given her so much joy.

With the passage of time Anne slowed down. She lightened her course load, spent more time reading than teaching, and eventually her heart was worn out and she was forced to retire.

On a blustery afternoon in late autumn, as she was watching *Northanger Abbey* on Masterpiece Theatre, she felt a sharp pain in her chest. She reached for the bottle of nitroglycerin that was always on the table next to her chair, and she placed a pill under her tongue. As the pain subsided, she became aware of a scratching at her door.

"Who is it?" she called. Slowly, with tired limbs attached to a tired body, she shuffled to the front door.

"Who is it?" she called again.

Receiving no answer, she opened the door. At first she thought no one was there. Then she felt something silky touching her bedroom-slippered feet and looked down. The white cat with the misshapen ear and tail walked in.

"Oh, my," Anne said, and she returned to her chair. When she had sat down, the cat jumped into her lap. Anne patted his head and scratched his rump. He purred and rubbed the top of his head all over her chin, and he licked her nose with his soft tongue. The cat and Anne gazed into each other's eyes, speaking wordless epics of love. She had another pain in her chest.

As Anne was reaching for the bottle of nitroglycerin, her heart stopped beating.

*

Visitors to the cemetery are excited to tell of the two women that are spotted on occasion in the distance, one of whom is always carrying a white cat in her arms. The women are observed strolling and talking, and when people turn for a second look they are gone. Although they are often seen in the cemetery, no one has ever seen them in the town. No one has ever gotten close enough to talk to them.

Acknowledgments

"Beach Shanty." Original to this volume.

"The Beldame." First published in *Illumen Magazine* (Spring 2023).

"Botched Job." Original to this volume.

"Cataclysm." Original to this volume.

"The Color of Magic." Original to this volume.

"Cosplay." Original to this volume.

"The Devil's Own." Original to this volume.

"Dolly." First published in *The Little Book of Cursed Dolls,* ed. Christa Coleridge (Media Macabre, 2023).

"Felinicity." Original to this volume.

"The Grey House." Original to this volume.

"Haunted House." Original to this volume.

"Holiday Shopping." Original to this volume.

"The House." Original to this volume.

"In the Shadow of Castle Dracula." First published in *A Tale That Is Told: The 50th Anniversary Anthology of the Dracula Society,* ed. Tracy Lee and Maria Weidmann (Dracula Society, 2023).

"Inspiration." Original to this volume.

"Inspired by Nature." Original to this volume.

"Invitation to Danse." First published in *JOURN-E: The Journal of Imaginative Literature* 3, No. 1 (Vernal Equinox 2024).

"Lady of the Lake." Original to this volume.

"Leave My Cat Alone!" First published in *Lycanthropicon: Imaginings & Images of the Werewolf* (Mind's Eye Publications, 2024).

"Lenore." First published in *Mensa Bulletin* (October 2021).

"Lila in Arcadia." Original to this volume.

"Lunar Mission." First published in *Spectral Realms* No. 20 (Winter 2024).

"Madeline." First published in in *JOURN-E: The Journal of Imaginative Literature* 2, No. 1 (Vernal Equinox 2023).

"The Magic Crystal Ball." Original to this volume.

"The Moon Is Made of Cat." First published in *Spectral Realms* No. 20 (Winter 2024).

"A Much-Needed Rest." Original to this volume.

"Out of This World." Original to this volume.

"Poor Winona." First published in *Jessica's Recurring Nightmares: Anthology of the Great Lakes Association of Horror Writers,* ed. M. C. St. John and J. M. Van Horn (Great Lakes Association of Horror Writers, 2023).

"Programmed." First published in *Trembling with Fear* (10 April 2022).

"Snowed In." Original to this volume.

"Stray Gods and Cats." Original to this volume.

"A Successful Woman Writer." Original to this volume.

"Till Death Reunite Us." Original to this volume.

"To Necrophilia." First published in *Horror Writers Association Poetry Showcase, Vol. VIII,* ed. Stephanie M. Wytovich (Horror Writers Association, October 2021).

"The Witch." First published in *Spectral Realms* No. 19 (Summer 2023).

———

I wish to thank these most marvelous friends without whom this volume would never have been published. Foremost, my best friends and brilliant horror authors Amanda Desiree and Michael Potts, as well as Joyce Nelson, the friend of a lifetime, and Deb Cirino, who have come to my rescue whenever I have flagged in my journey through the Unnamable Abysses of Publishing, who have served as the principal readers and critics of my unending stream of writing, and who have been my dearest friends in every way imaginable. As well my *Dark Shadows* friends Frank Bell and Joe Escobar, who have repeatedly wished me well and urged me forward in my literary endeavors. And, finally, my own Professor Armitage, S. T. Joshi, Mentor Nonpareil, who has offered me untold opportunities to learn the publishing trade, who has guided me in my Lovecraftian studies, and who understands and esteems cats as much as I do.

www.ingramcontent.com/pod-product-compliance
Lightning Source LLC
Chambersburg PA
CBHW071955170626
46813CB00005B/1887